Sarah swallowed, her shivering body urging her mind to relinquish those last shreds of propriety which seemed so hopelessly out of place suddenly. "I want you to love me."

"I do — I will." Augusta's hands began to move again then, trailing over Sarah's front with a bold pressure that made her gasp. She in turn pressed closer to Augusta's warmth, biting back a surge of nervous panic. She trailed her fingers along either side of Augusta's spine, and felt the quick tightening of muscle there.

Augusta, too, shuddered with pleasure, then looped the bedclothes around them both and rolled onto the pillows. She pulled Sarah along, the last bits of restrictive clothing tumbling from between them. Sarah felt an insistent tongue slip along her tender throat, and instinctively locked her knees around Augusta's. She felt the curve of a smile transform Augusta's kiss against her shoulder.

"As when we danced," she whispered into yielding flesh. "I have much to teach you, Miss Lindsay."

"There is much I wish to learn."

Passion's Legacy

BY LORI A. PAIGE

Passion's Legacy

BY LORI A. PAIGE

The Naiad Press, Inc.
1991

Printed in the United States of America on acid-free paper
First Edition

Edited by Christine Cassidy
Cover design by Pat Tong and Bonnie Liss
    (Phoenix Graphics)
Typeset by Sandi Stancil

Library of Congress Cataloging-in-Publication Data

Paige, Lori A., 1965—
    Passion's legacy / by Lori A. Paige.
        p.   cm.
    ISBN 0-941483-81-9 : $8.95
    I. Title.
PS3566.A3395P3   1991
813'.54--dc20   90-21997
                                                          CIP

DEDICATION

In keeping with our literature's tradition of celebrating women's strength, I would like to dedicate this publication to the memory of my grandmother, Maria Schröeder (1898–1989). She was, in fact, the strongest woman I have ever known, and, not coincidentally, the most-loved. She was a feisty German who never shied from expressing an opinion on anything that affected her, and I will always regret that I could not put this finished product into her hands.

I would also like to thank Jane, a compatriot in nine years' worth of mischief, and Jo, with whom I share a pleasant home, for manuscript suggestions.

ABOUT THE AUTHOR

I am a native New Englander who has lived happily in the Pioneer Valley of Western Massachusetts for the past seven years. During the first four of these, I attended Smith College, from which I received the Maya Yates Writing Prize upon graduation in May, 1987. I am currently pursuing a Ph.D. in Victorian Literature from the University of Massachusetts in Amherst, and hope to enjoy an academic career which will encompass both scholarly pursuits and creative writing (which I have been working at since third grade, when I typed my first fifteen-page extravaganza).

PROLOGUE

May 15, 1815:

Emilia Lindsay screamed again, wringing her hands through the rails of the headboard. Her prison bars, thought Catherine. The sounds of agony ripped at her soul with the force of a cleaver. Emilia's swollen body bucked.

"She's fighting me," she choked, her fingers clawing at Catherine's hands. "It's a judgment, Cathy."

"No, dearest, no!" Catherine's tears ran down her

nose freely. She pressed closer to Emilia, as if to absorb some of her friend's pain by proximity. The front of Emilia's nightdress was gray with sweat. "It's childbirth is all. It tortures everyone the same."

"Well, I don't want to live. What use? Lionel will never forgive me . . ."

"Never mind Lionel. What of your child? Emilia, I shan't turn from you. I'm not like Samuel. Please, dearest, listen to me, and be strong."

"Can't. Can't. I curse Samuel. Don't ever let him take this child." Her mouth contorted with hatred as well as suffering. "Not that he'd want it. Bastard. Liar." Another contortion rocked her. "Oh, Cathy, any time now, I know it."

"Lionel is coming with the midwife." He had gone fifteen miles in the rain to fetch her. No doctor, though it was clear his sister faced a difficult birth. Doctors gossiped. Midwives could be bought. "Shall I go and call for him?"

"Yes, yes, please. Oh, what horror. I welcome death just now." She began shivering wildly. Catherine leaped up and flung open the door. *Damn this fine country home, so isolated as to be hellish now. Another example of Lionel Lindsay's discretion.*

The single serving-maid they had engaged from the village came running. "Is it time, then?" she asked breathlessly, her Gaelic red hair standing on end from the screams.

"Yes, it must be. Please run out, Annie, and try and see them. Make them hurry. Emilia hasn't much strength left . . ."

Annie gulped and raced out to the drive.

Catherine rushed back to Emilia, choking back her own sobs as she ran. Emilia, slipping rapidly into delirium, was extending an unsteady arm to her. "Stay with me, Cathy. Stay with me."

Catherine did stay. She forced herself to talk, to distract Emilia as best she could. She wasn't sure what she talked about: names for the child, a Scarborough resort they would visit when Emilia was well again, scandals at court she had read in the newssheets. It was all one to Emilia.

Finally, twenty minutes later, Lionel and his midwife burst in. The midwife took immediate charge, banishing Catherine to the sitting room. Lionel had to drag her out. Annie was called in to assist instead. Catherine was livid.

"Miss Hudson, I must insist you control your emotions!" Lionel's white neck strained against his stiff collar. "We have bedlam enough as it is!"

"Well you ought to feel guilty," Catherine hissed. "This is your doing, Lionel, as surely as it is Samuel's."

"Complete nonsense! I did not introduce them. You have your fine cousin Andrew to thank for that."

"It was you who forced her into wooing at all! She was happy enough by herself —"

"With you, you mean." Lionel's expression turned sour. "Girlhood friendships must give way to something more permanent, Miss Hudson. If my realism makes me an ogre to your attitude, so be it."

"Your realism is about to kill your sister," Catherine shot back. Then, sinking into a chair, she began to cry desperately. Lionel walked stiffly to the big windows overlooking the west pasture, folded his hands behind his back and bent his head in silence.

The midwife emerged close to an hour later. Catherine saw the splotches of blood on her hands.

"The child is safe," she informed Lionel. "Annie's taken it out. Your sister . . ."

She did not have to go on. "I see," Lionel said. Catherine bolted for Emilia before they could prepare her. The sheets and floor were slimy with blood. Emilia lay back, deflated, her eyes uncomprehending and her breath ragged.

Catherine covered her slack face with kisses.

"Couldn't be strong any longer," Emilia apologized. She lasted only a few minutes more.

Lionel pulled Catherine to her feet and guided her into the garden. The rain had slowed, and both Lionel and Catherine needed the fresh air. Catherine wanted to gouge out his eyes.

"I will have someone take you to the village in two days' time, Miss Hudson. You will not want to stay past the funeral."

"I want the child," Catherine said.

"Out of the question! Your parents would never allow it, for one thing. For another, you yourself are unmarried."

"Don't speak to me of parental concern. Where are yours, after all?"

"I concede that their attitude is . . . unfortunate. I have done all I could. Surely you realize that."

"I do." Catherine sighed. She covered her face, the tears flooding out once again. "But I want the little girl, Lionel. I'll take care of her somehow . . ."

"Miss Hudson, on the whole I think it would be better if you did not see the child at all."

She jumped to her feet. "You can't mean that!"

"I think it would be best, in fact. You cannot possibly care for her. I, at least, have the means and the legal right to her."

"You mean to keep her?" Catherine couldn't believe it. After all Lionel's railing against the bastard who was about to sully his impeccable family name? After his parents' complete repudiation of their only daughter, right up to her dying hour? "What hypocrisy, Lionel!"

"I prefer to call it prudence. Perhaps you should go to the village tonight. I will fetch you for the funeral. By then, the child will be on its way home. This country chill cannot be healthy for it anyhow."

He walked back into the house and called for a servant. Catherine heard him issue instructions to pack Miss Hudson's things and prepare a gig to carry her to the village inn. In the distance, the infant bawled. Catherine was ready to fly at him afresh when he returned to the garden. The only thing that stopped her was the sight of tears gushing over his own red cheeks.

September 5, 1824:

The young woman with the fire-colored tresses surveyed herself balefully. Corseted and curled, bejeweled and solemnly lectured, she was now considered ready to stride into the church and be claimed by her groom. If only her parents realized

5

how ridiculous all their muffled hints at how best to please Sir Lewis made them look! Yet she had listened and smiled, and feigned shock when convention required. Now that the morning of the wedding had arrived, she was filled with nothing so much as a sense of relief that a long pretense was ending. In their own home, she and Lewis could at last be themselves.

Her mother scurried around her even now, straightening a bit of lace, adding a spritz of scent to her hair. "Well, dear, your last day as an Ivors. I can scarcely believe it. And you the last among your sisters . . . When you were little I kept thinking we'd have you forever."

Augusta laughed. "You'd only have wanted me if I'd stayed little."

"Well, of course we couldn't have you becoming a spinster . . . I am sorry if you felt we were pushing you last Season. It was never that we didn't want you, Gussie. But what sort of life can a woman have by herself? We were thinking of you always. I'm sure Sir Lewis will be kind to you. He's a good, decent man . . . if a bit old for you."

"He's well-settled in the world, though. That's an advantage a younger man couldn't offer."

"Thirty-four isn't so ancient, I suppose. People are living longer every decade, your father says." She sighed. "Now, where is that silly maid with your earring? We can't stand about all day. I'll die of the frets."

Augusta felt insidious. "Shall I bellow for her?" she asked sweetly. Her mother was mortified.

"Augusta Jane! Didn't I tell you never to do that again once you're married? Your own household staff and you acting like that . . ." She blustered about until the maid appeared with the hastily mended earring. Augusta bent down and felt it slide into place.

"There." Margaret Ivors actually applauded. "Ready with time to spare. Lady Pym, I can't believe it."

The ceremony progressed much as Augusta expected. Sir Lewis, likewise scrubbed and humbled, flashed her a kind smile as she took her place beside him. The wedding band offset her other rings prettily. The oaths they took had a particular poignancy. They were indeed one another's protection.

A lavish wedding luncheon followed the ceremony. As she stood by her husband, their arms loosely joined, Augusta caught sight of a pair of intense eyes that sparkled like emeralds. The eyes were attached to a small blonde woman, perhaps a year or two younger than Augusta. Wearing the most expensive gown present, she accompanied an equally striking mother. Augusta recognized the older woman as an occasional guest of Margaret's.

Releasing Sir Lewis, she muttered an excuse about paying her respects and crossed the room to greet them. Mrs. Finch looked surprised that a bride should be so forthright in presenting herself. Nevertheless, she seemed to realize that Gussie had a reputation for unorthodoxy that many considered charming. Sir Lewis apparently did.

"I'm so pleased you could come, Mrs. Finch." Augusta stuck out her gloved hand. "And your daughter."

Mrs. Finch flushed with pleasure as she scooted

her child forward. "You've not met her yet because she's been away at school. Devon, you know. They have the finest curriculum. Even taught riding one day a week."

"Very useful." Augusta nodded.

Miss Finch, one golden brow cocked defiantly, dipped a vague curtsy. "Congratulations on your marriage, Lady Pym. I hope you shall be very happy." Her tone was anything but sincere.

Augusta's smile broadened. "May I borrow your daughter, Mrs. Finch? My husband ought to have the pleasure of meeting her too."

"Oh, delighted, delighted." Mrs. Finch's head bobbed with enthusiasm, as if she had worried that Isabel's caustic manner would render her a social disaster . . .

CHAPTER 1

"Happy birthday, my dear Sarah. Please, stay a moment. I hope you won't think me too impudent if I offer you somewhat prematurely the gift I've brought you." Ian Hyde's tall form hovered over her, his lips parting to reveal the long-toothed, rather insinuating smile which had somehow managed to captivate her Uncle Lionel in the brief interval of thirteen months. Finding herself trapped between the dining room, where her uncle had chanced to detain her for a moment, and the drawing room, where she was about to follow their female guests into retirement, she had no choice but to endure his attentions as he reached into his emerald tailcoat and produced an oblong box which had been covered in the identical fabric. "And here it is." He held it before her with a flourish. "I have almost every confidence you will approve of it."

"My uncle's approval ought perhaps to concern you more," she murmured self-consciously, her eyes seeking in vain the closed doors of the two rooms for any welcome interruption. Still, she had no intention of allowing Mr. Hyde to believe that she relished further conversation with him, nor any of the obligations even the simplest of gifts from a gentleman might incur.

"Nonsense," he went on, "I've already spoken with him. I even presented the actual gift for inspection, and may I say that he was most impressed with its quality and value."

"Please, Mr. Hyde, could it not wait until later this evening? I should hate to offend our other guests by appearing too partial to any one of you."

His smile broadened. Brushing a lock of glossy dark hair from his tall forehead, he pressed the box toward her. "I could not presume your favoritism — merely your indulgence in accepting this, a token of my inestimable regard for you. So here, my precious Miss Lindsay, please take it. I daresay Uncle Lionel might be far more offended if you did not."

Sarah hesitated, then sighed and allowed him to wrap her fingers around the box. Ian was correct in assuming she had no desire to inflame her Uncle Lionel. Though infrequent, his rages were not pleasant. And he had glanced at her in an unusual, rather unnerving manner several times in the course of the dinner he had offered in honor of her twenty-second birthday.

"The fabric is pleasant to stroke," he prompted, when her fingers did not immediately seek the clasp, "but I promise you shall find the contents even more intriguing. Open it now."

"Very well." Sarah carefully set her facial expression into one of gravity and distance. To placate Uncle Lionel, she would humor his overbearing, middle-aged friend. The box's contents sparkled in the candlelight's amber wash as she gradually exposed them. Before she found her voice, Ian lifted the necklace in his slim white fingers and held it before her.

"You are impressed." He nodded with satisfaction. "I knew you would be. And, if you won't begrudge me the compliment, I will venture to say it shall look stunning on you. Allow me."

He had started to fasten it around her throat. The cold clasp bit at her bare shoulder. She jumped.

"No . . . I don't think you should, Mr. Hyde."

"And why not?" His black eyes grew icy. "The piece is worthless unless it is worn, you know."

"But it's so . . . valuable," she improvised. "I couldn't keep such a thing in good conscience. Not unless it came from a relation, at least."

"I told you your uncle had no objections on that score. You are not implying, I hope, that I cannot afford extravagant gifts for those who mean most to me?" Ignoring her gasp of surprise, he seized her by the arms, spun her around, and snapped the clasp shut. It felt rather too tight. Hyde whirled her around again, admiring his purchase.

"An admirable fit. Wear it one hour, Miss

11

Lindsay, and then return it to the box if you still feel that you must. I think, though, you will have grown more attached to it by then."

If she slapped his face now, as she had every inclination to do, she'd have the devil to pay in the guise of her uncle. The idea of dropping Ian Hyde's precious jewels and knocking them aside with her heel was, however, very appealing.

She settled for flashing an unpleasant smile. "Very well, I'll do you the honor this once, Mr. Hyde. And thank you for your gift."

He dropped a mock bow. "Though it pains me, I must thank your kind uncle and take my leave now. I shall be riding back to Salisbury tonight, and it is no short journey. Not, of course, that I was unwilling to make the sacrifice. Good night . . . though I trust you will think of me again this evening." His fingers brushed her hand once, and he left her. Sarah bolted for the drawing room.

The buzz of feminine conversation met her at the door. Before entering, she yanked off the necklace and stashed the closed box behind a bronze figurine in the foyer. Assuming a nonchalant smile, she stepped among the circle of overdressed matrons. The oldest, and largest, of them rose.

"Here she is at last." Mrs. Chathley held out a gloved hand which Sarah was not expected to grasp. "Your uncle certainly must have had a good deal to say to you, to keep you from us this long!"

"You must tell us everything he said. Providing it wasn't terribly personal, of course." Lady Larken sounded hopeful.

"It was actually a matter of small consequence," Sarah hedged. Just the usual reminders to thank and flatter their guests before they disbanded, she thought. Uncle Lionel had never given her credit for mastering the most rudimentary social skills. He still thought of her as the squealing ten-year-old who had dashed into a full drawing room with muddied feet and presented Lady Hiema Kestle with a writhing pink earthworm.

"Well, I'll wager it concerned a suitor." Mrs. Emmeline Massey, crusted over with jewelry, arched her back against the divan. "After all, one's birthday is an eminently suitable time to advance a claim. And you are certainly of age, my dear. Had you not been such a sickly child, you would have been married before now. And if Lionel didn't fear living alone once again."

"I don't think he'd resent the aloneness." Sarah had chosen a seat near the windows. The fact that this same idea had occurred to her, particularly after the encounter with Mr. Hyde, offered no comfort. "But I'm in no hurry to wed, as you know."

"That's because you live with an old celibate," Mrs. Chathley stated. Emmeline Massey gasped.

"No," Sarah said. In truth, her enthusiasm had begun to wane as soon as she'd realized how little the realities of matchmaking resembled the rose-scented courtships and summertime strolls she had envisioned in younger days. When she had been forced to contemplate what everyone declared was inevitable anyway, she had imagined herself at least pledging fidelity and obedience to a trim, doe-eyed squire's son, and not the aging squire himself. The promenade through their home of her uncle's pockmarked, gout-ridden friends had sent her from the dinner table with a sour stomach more than

13

once. She remembered the swollen pale warts on the joints of Mr. Alston's left fingers as he'd refilled her wine glass last Christmas Eve. He had rambled about Princess Victoria's recent fortuitous escape from the fever. "Not," he'd added smugly, "that she had nothing to fight for."

"But really, we mustn't be too hard on the men," Lady Larken was saying in an affected tone, apparently responding to some comment which Sarah, preoccupied, had not heard. "Without us to guide them, they'd be one writhing mass of blistered flesh, sliding down to the fire-pits." When this comment provoked giggles, she forged ahead with great certainty. "You've all see that horrible painting Sir Devon Rothand keeps in his study? Well, every day I praise my Maker for sparing our sex such wretched, lustful impulses."

Emmeline nodded. "Beyond the men to see it, of course." She sipped her small glass of port, pursing her lips in appreciation. "That's the real tragedy of being the male of any species."

A scandalized titter floated around the group. Sarah was the only one who did not join in.

"We're embarrassing Miss Lindsay," Lady Larken warned. "She couldn't possibly know what brutes they can be in their passions. Perhaps we'd best not disillusion her."

"Well, not always brutes," Mrs. Chathley admitted. "But I have been forced to roll my eyes in disgust once in a while, I can tell you that."

"I presume you've heard about Sir Timothy and his newest actress?"

"No! Has he another? I would have thought that

after that scene during Lady Stephanie's hunting weekend . . ."

The women launched into a gossipy discussion of this scandal. Sarah, turning back to the window, soon lost the thread entirely. Was it so impossible, truly, for a woman to feel passion? If this were the case, what hope could she hold out for ever making a tolerable match? To share anything like mutual respect or companionable regard with the likes of Mr. Hyde or any of his peers seemed worse than ludicrous. And the younger dandies she had encountered at various parties and balls, though more pleasant to look at, had always failed to stir either her heart or her imagination. There was more to courtship, perhaps, than she was able to recognize. Mrs. Massey squeezed her hand.

"Don't let us spoil your fancies. At your age they're appallingly essential. Whomever your uncle finds for you, I'm certain you'll fare marvelously. Haven't we all?"

A servant suddenly entered the room, preceding Mr. Chathley. After greeting the other ladies, he turned a flippant half-bow to his wife. "Time we were rolling, my girl. Can't risk a chill, now, can we?" Sarah noticed, as he spoke, that his own cheeks were amply flushed with wine and mirth. Mrs. Chathley boldly pinched them.

"You're the one who had best cover yourself," she laughed, sneaking a wink at Lady Larken. "Off with you, then, we'll just take our leave of Lionel."

The departure of the first couple proved a decorous cue for the other guests, and when Sarah had weathered the last of the birthday kisses and insincere invitations to tea, she turned away with relief and a sudden longing for the stillness of her room and the crisp linen of the bed which awaited her. "If you'll excuse me, Uncle . . ."

The blunt pressure of his fingers on her forearm stopped her. "One moment, dear child. Will you join me in the study for a moment? I know well that you're tired."

Sarah allowed herself to be led into the dark-paneled study. Lionel graciously pulled up a chair for her, then settled himself behind his own imposing desk. A long Oriental tapestry hung on the wall just behind his head; somehow it seemed to frame his stocky, imposing figure, the splashes of gold and vermilion bringing out the orangish highlights in his crisp, curling hair and whiskers. Propping his elbows on the blotter, he rubbed his hands together in thought, his eyes following the flashes of his diamond rings in the candlelight.

"Well, Sarah," he said finally, lacing his blunt fingers. "I trust your birthday celebrations pleased you?"

"You are referring to Mr. Hyde's generous gift?" She had dropped her façade of docility when the last guest had vanished; her sarcasm, uncorked, flooded her conversation.

"Then you did receive it. I wondered. You are not wearing it."

"You detained me so that he could present it."

Uncle Lionel shrugged. He rarely felt required to justify himself to his niece.

Her temper flashed. "I do not intend ever to wear it. His gifts are not welcome. Especially not gifts of jewelry. Jewelry of any sort."

16

He was not pleased. "Each time you gain a year, Sarah, you feel entitled to speak even more directly. It is not becoming."

"Yes, I know you prefer delicacy and decorum." She lisped the words and tipped her head to the ceiling.

"Yes, I always have, Sarah, and honor most of all. Yet I have never begrudged you your intelligence. Even you must admit that I've fostered it as best I could. Your outbursts are its overflow. My recognition of that fact allows me to excuse them, whereas many would not."

"Even if it will make my life unnecessarily complicated."

"Parrot me if you wish, but you'll see that I am right. The ignorant are often the most comfortable in this world. But you weren't born stupid, and I know an iron boot hasn't straightened a crooked limb yet."

They had jammed Lord Byron's leg in an iron boot, she recalled. His own mother had watched the screw being tightened. Springing from this cruel trap, ultimately, had been both a clubbed foot and an embittered and tormented child who had become an iconoclastic, and, most agreed, deviant man. No, her uncle and Lady Byron were not of a kind, and for that she was indeed thankful. But then, she was far from an aristocratic poet herself.

"Uncle, you have raised me as your own offspring, a consideration I have never, and never shall, take for granted. I have, I swear to you, never failed to remember you in my prayers for your charity and your affection. And it is those qualities I appeal to most at this moment. Do not darken the entire remainder of my life by joining it to that of

17

Ian Hyde. I could never care for him. I can scarcely bring myself to respect him."

"Ian is a principled man, in his own manner, and I am given to understand that other women have found him to their taste. But —" he waved an arm as if to dismiss the conflict these contrasting views presented to his own intellect — "who can account for women's attitudes? Since you beseech me so affectingly, I shan't press the matter. I am not, it is true, your father, and therefore I cannot presume to force you into any union of my arrangement. But I would ask a consideration from you in return."

"My deepest thanks, Uncle. You have no idea what relief your words afford me. And whatever favor I have the power to grant, you may indeed consider yours."

"What I ask is merely this: you are intelligent enough, and ethical enough, to understand honor, a responsibility which I, as master of my household, must never forsake. You therefore must try to see this matter of your betrothal as I am forced to."

Sarah felt a slow flush creep up the back of her neck. "Oh?" She feigned nonchalance, shifting her eyes coolly onto Uncle Lionel's blotter. "Am I a source of embarrassment to you then, Uncle? I must admit I fail to see how —"

"Sarah, you may remain a much happier young lady if you ceased to pursue this line of inquiry now. I will not deceive you, but I will caution you that my most truthful answers cannot help but ultimately distress you. Shall we say goodnight, then? Mr. Hyde's suit is no longer your concern. I shall inform him so myself to spare you further embarrassment."

Lionel moved uncomfortably, as if to stand.

Sarah, however, remained rigid in her velvet-backed chair. Her eyes now met his, and he was the one who flinched first.

"If I have shamed you, Uncle, I would prefer to confront my failings now. As I've said, I have been grateful for your charity. I should now be grateful for an equal portion of veracity."

Lionel resumed his seat, laced his fingers, and stared again at his rings. "These words do not come easily to me, Sarah. I would not have you think that they did, when you reflect on this moment for all the rest of your years."

"Proceed," she said coldly.

"Very well. Perhaps you have wondered, now and again, why we have in fact waited so long to contract your marriage. After all, you are twenty-two now; most of the young ladies you were once pleased to consort with were wedded and bedded years ago. Yet you remain."

"I had assumed it was because you enjoyed my presence here, particularly after Aunt's death. Then there was my illness . . ."

"These things are both true. Yet many young women have married within a year of surviving even the pox. No, Sarah, we have waited so long because we wished to observe you, as you grew older. We wished to be certain —" he wrung his fingers in what seemed close to embarrassment. "Forgive me, Sarah, but we wished to be sure you would not turn out in your adulthood to be the sort of woman that might indeed cause us pain. In short, the sort of woman your mother was."

"My mother?" The heat on her neck blazed now, surging out into her shoulders, and, she was all too certain, onto her cheeks and forehead. "My mother herself died of the pox before she had scarcely had a chance to be a woman. You told me yourself. And my poor father with her."

"That your parents are both dead is true enough. However, we cannot be certain the pox was responsible. It may have been some ailment far more disgraceful, for all we know. They did not die together, as we have led you to believe. In fact, they never saw one another after your birth . . . nor several months beforehand, if I recall correctly. It has been some time, and I have honestly tried to push the entire matter from my mind."

He rubbed his own forehead, perhaps prompted by the scarlet stain spreading on hers. Realizing she had, for the moment, been struck dumb, he hurried on. "When your mother was eighteen, she too rebelled against the perfectly acceptable match contracted for her by our parents. One night, after a party, she disappeared from the house with a rakish young naval officer she had met no more than three weeks before. We were frantic, of course, and inquired after her to no little expense and humiliation. When she returned, she brought you with her, in an unborn state of course — and, need I mention, she wore no ring. Her friend, of course, had better sense. He accepted the bride chosen by his own parents for him, and volunteered a yearly sum toward your upkeep provided you did not take his name. Thus we always told you that you were the product of a marriage between distant cousins, doubly a Lindsay."

"When in truth I am not one at all," she murmured softly. Her blush was gone now, and instead she sat white and bathed in clammy sweat. "No, Sarah. I loved my sister as well as could any brother under the circumstances. And you have proven yourself far better than she. But now you see my dilemma. The truth of your parentage would of course be revealed in any marital contract; not all suitors would be as gracious as Mr. Hyde in overlooking the blemish."

"Mr. Hyde knows, then?" Her eyes widened in horror.

"Rest assured his discretion is absolute. I could scarcely have encouraged him under false pretenses, dearest. You realize that."

She rose slowly, keeping one hand clenched around the chair arm. "You have wounded me greatly, Uncle."

"I tried to forewarn you —"

"No, you mistake my meaning. It is better that I know. And you were correct: I do understand honor. You will forgive my shock, though, now that you have informed me I can really have none."

"Come, Sarah, that's not so." Lionel stood too, extending a hand to her. Yet she knew he did not really want her to take it, nor would she have considered it anyhow. "I don't hold you to blame for what occurred before you were born! No one has ever suggested, nor ever will, that I have raised you improperly. As for your suitors, you can barely blame them for . . ."

"I blame no one, just as no one would blame you

for declining to purchase Mr. Rolfson's colt last night at dinner. After it is born, you told him. Not before. I . . . admire your foresight, Uncle. Now goodnight."

"That is a very insensitive comparison. I am a businessman, Sarah."

"Indeed you are, Uncle. I must go now. Surely you understand."

"I shall see you upstairs."

"No." At last she was able to lift her hand from the chair arm, and she held it out sternly before her to ward him away. "Please wait until I am gone."

"As you wish." She heard the sadness in his voice, but now it failed to move her. It could, after all, be nothing compared to her own. Nothing.

She closed the door behind her.

CHAPTER 2

The idea came to her in the middle of what proved, not surprisingly, to be an unpleasant, uncertain sleep. It began as a fancy, suggested in a floating dream by some anonymous, threatening character, who trilled about cool green islands, black rocks, and lakes so deep even sunken ships could not be recovered. By the time she had propped herself up on her elbows, a tangle of cold sweaty hair in her eyes, she had formed the determination to leave. For the rest of the night, she rehearsed the announcement of her plan, which she would make over breakfast.

When she entered the morning-hall, therefore, she wasted no time, asking the cook for very strong tea and downing it without flinching.

Uncle Lionel appeared not long afterward. He had taken much time over his attire that morning, since he was riding into Salisbury for an appointment. He wore a tiny but valuable sapphire in his cravat. This had been a gift from Sarah several Christmases ago. She knew he had worn it to placate her, to remind her of the bond that continued between them despite last night's harsh words. Perhaps he even hoped she had forgotten the details of their confrontation.

He moved to brush his lips across her forehead, an uncharacteristic gesture he performed with a kind of resigned embarrassment. She smelled the sweet hair tonic which held his curls in careful disarray. When he stared at her, she shuddered. Were the humiliating images that had flickered through her mind all night apparent in her expression? A grubby roadside tavern, her mother howling, naked, on a bare mattress with a half-dressed man lounging beside her . . . On her teacup were five damp spots where her fingers had been.

"I feel as if I'm near starvation." Lionel made a half-hearted attempt at flippancy. "One of the drawbacks of a fine, heavy dinner."

"Uncle," she spoke evenly, quietly, "I should like to go on holiday."

"What's this?"

"I should like to leave here as quickly as

possible, and I should like to remain away for perhaps five weeks. I must of course request your assistance with the preparations; I hope you shan't begrudge me the favor. If the money must come from my dowry, I shall not be resentful. In fact, if necessity did not compel me to ask this, I should not presume on your generosity."

"Sarah, where do you get these whims? You said nothing yesterday —"

"Yesterday," she said bluntly, staring him full in the face, "things were much different between us. I can no longer bide here with such . . . circumstances weighing upon me."

"I made it clear to you last night that my feelings for you can never, and will never, alter. If any coldness has arisen between us, I suggest you look into your own heart to smother the source."

"At present, Uncle, I cannot possibly look into my heart, for the shame I should encounter there would no doubt prove more fatal than the pox. Time, perhaps, is our only possible physician in this case. If indeed my life is at all dear to you, Uncle, you shall not deny me this physic. And I know you are not a cruel man."

The cook's assistant entered the room, bearing dishes. Lionel did not speak until they were alone again. "No doubt you feel your proposal is eminently rational. Yet you expect me to let you travel on your own, with every harbor filled with thieves, and our cities stinking with more vice than a millworker's privy? I'm afraid I cannot compliment your forethought, which seems nonexistent in this case."

"I am not unwilling to repay your faith in me,

Uncle. I . . . am no longer the proud creature you addressed last night, you see." She stirred her sugarless tea.

"Repay me?" His lower lip curled stubbornly as she lifted the dishcovers and began filling his plate. "You have nothing I want, save for your filial affections."

"If you would do me this favor, I would grant you a similar consideration."

"Meaning?"

"Meaning while I am away, I will . . . attempt to reconsider Mr. Hyde's attentions. I cannot promise acquiescence, but I do promise that I will no longer treat him so . . . haughtily."

A long silence ensued, punctuated only by the clatter of Lionel's silverware as he feasted. Sarah sat very still, her hands motionless in her lap.

"Well!" Lionel snorted at last.

That afternoon, he sent a letter to his reputable friend Mrs. Elizabeth Waterbury, requesting that she receive his niece at her fashionable townhouse in Bath.

Sarah and Lionel had little to converse about as they stood by the small trap which would transport Sarah, her maid, and their luggage to the coachstop near Stourbury, three miles off. Lionel, the lines around his eyes looking darker and deeper than usual, pressed her hand with his doeskin-gloved hand.

"I shall write when I arrive."

"Yes," he said. He turned to Valerie Dobbins, the

upstairs maid whom Sarah had chosen, somewhat to his distaste, as her traveling companion. Valerie dropped a brief, eager curtsy. Like their other servants, she preferred to keep Mr. Lionel happy rather than scoff at the petty deferences he expected.

He handed her a coin. "I shall expect no less than your complete reliability and diligent service to my niece," he said sternly.

"I'll do my best, sir." Her brown eyes implored him for his trust.

"Well, then." Lionel stepped away. Sarah climbed into the trap, Valerie settling opposite her. She signaled, and they lurched down the drive. Lionel paced alongside them until they turned into the street.

Like the house, the front garden, and the familiar village shops, he soon dropped out of sight. When they passed into a more rural section, Sarah stared at the blur of stone walls, stubbly trees, and sheep. Valerie did not intrude on what were obviously brooding thoughts. She endured the jolts and shakings of the uneven road in silence. When they reached Stourbury, a solemn gray drizzle had just begun to silver the sky.

They shared the coach with three other travelers: a bespectacled young woman whose wobbling pile of books and studious expression proclaimed her a governess or schoolmistress; an older man, in finely cut but rumpled clothes, whose big head, mostly hairless, dipped and rolled in an uncertain slumber against the seat-back for an hour at a time; and a tall young man in a dark blue suit and beautiful black whiskers, who gestured as he talked with a hand bearing a prominent gold wedding band. The rain was worse now, lashing against the carriage with enough fury to shake the old gentleman wide awake at fairly frequent intervals.

"Driver says we may have to stop soon," the young man said, gesturing, climbing back into his seat after a brief stop to refresh the horses. "Mud's getting fierce, he tells me."

"It does sound quite dreadful out." Sarah looked up to the patch of sky she could see past the narrow window. A good deal of moisture had seeped in through it, and stained the coach interior a musty brown. Valerie was eyeing the same spot, never speaking.

"I, for one, would sooner stop than overturn ourselves in some wretched puddle," the governess observed, the lack of light now making her reading a less comfortable pursuit. "I have no desire to arrive in Bath looking as though I'd walked the entire distance."

The elderly man, roused again from his obstinate slumber, sputtered some agreement. Just then the carriage slashed through a particularly vicious puddle, and its entire frame tilted harshly to one side. Valerie slammed sideways against Sarah, the governess's book flew out of her hand, and the man in the blue suit rolled into the elderly gentleman, who unexpectedly barked out a curse. When they had recovered, and had resumed their regular seats, his pale cheeks were reddening.

"My apologies to the ladies, of course."

"You'll never catch me uttering such careless sentiments in a crisis," the young man laughed. "No telling where one might end up in the very next instant."

"Well taken, well taken, sir," the old man puffed in extreme humiliation. Valerie, looking down, was smiling.

Presently they rolled to another stop. The blue-suited man stood, preparing to push his way outside for another word with their driver, but the driver forestalled him by coming around to peer through the window himself. Sarah was startled at the man's appearance: the mud was trickling down both sides of his nose, his clothes were saturated, and even his voice was raspy and rough with damp and cold. He was unwrapping his thick muffler to bare his mouth and chin as he spoke.

"We'll not be goin' no further this evening. Road's solid muck ahead, from what I can tell. We'll stop at this inn tonight, carry on in the morning when I've had time to clear up these wheels, an' my beasties."

"Very sensible, it seems to me," said the governess.

"I suppose we're expected to pay for these temporary lodgings with our own funds," the elderly man said irritably.

The driver merely shrugged, replaced his muffler, and walked back out into the rain.

"Oh, come now, Mr. Martin." The young man shrugged cheerfully. "I welcome adventure — not to mention a respite from this nastiness. A fire and a strong draught sound very congenial right now."

"I was only thinking of the ladies." Mr. Martin

scowled, peering out at the inn. "This place looks scarcely respectable to me. 'The Rollicking Gull' indeed!"

"I'm sure we'll manage very nicely," Sarah could not forbear snapping, though she noticed a look of genuine uncertainty flicker in the governess's eyes. Still, the bookish woman gathered her things and resolutely climbed out with the others, who marched single-file across an incredibly swampy courtyard and into the only slightly more reassuring confines of The Rollicking Gull. Its lower level consisted of a low-ceilinged tavern, decorated with a few round pewter platters on the wall and filled with tables hosting burly, mud-splashed men who lifted tankards in a mock toast as the travelers filed in. The driver went to speak to the innkeeper.

The governess moved closer to Sarah. "I do hope you won't think me impossibly rude, Miss Lindsay, but I . . . that is to say, I wonder if perhaps you might be hesitant to engage a room on your own, in this unfamiliar place . . ."

"I shouldn't think you rude at all." Sarah nodded, her eyes on the leering male faces that seemed to surround them on every side.

"These small rustic communities . . ." the man in blue whispered to the group. "Basically harmless blokes, but with absolutely no sense when it comes to behaving like civilized men."

Rooms were engaged. Sarah and the governess agreed to adjoining chambers with a maid's cabinet for Valerie between them. A weather-beaten woman with dusky hair carried their cases upstairs, gesturing with her chin down an empty stretch of hall as they crossed the landing. "Now don't go wandering down there," she cautioned them. "Those rooms are private, reserved for a very fine lady and her people. That whole section's hers, mind you now."

"I'm sure we'll have no occasion to disturb her." Sarah lifted her brows in annoyance. Undoubtedly this fine lady had also been forced by the storm to detour to the Gull.

"Could you send us up something to eat?" the governess asked as they surveyed the room. "And a pot of strong tea, certainly."

"Yes'm," their hostess mumbled without enthusiasm, waiting by the door until Sarah gave her a coin.

When they were alone, the governess, who had since introduced herself as Miss Gwinn, flushed and reached for her own purse. "Please forgive me, Miss Lindsay, whatever must you think of me? I'm not terribly used to traveling, and I'm rather tired besides . . ."

"Never mind." Sarah was suddenly very tired herself. She sank down on her own bed as Valerie opened her smallest case.

"I'll just be laying your nightdress out, Miss."

"Yes, fine, then go and get some rest until the dinner arrives. We can put it there, perhaps." Sarah indicated an unpolished wooden table standing in the corner.

"I'll make it ready, then." Valerie moved away.

Sarah watched her with a vague curiosity. What thoughts did Valerie's subservient decorum really conceal . . . if any? Did she sometimes burn with anger, as Sarah did, lashing out only at herself in consequence? Never a defiant word to Uncle Lionel or Mr. Hyde, and for Valerie, never a defiant word to Sarah herself. But in the privacy of her intellect . . .

Miss Gwinn was saying something about starting a letter to a fellow teacher at the school she had just left. She was, she'd explained, en route to her mother's house in Bath to help nurse a younger sibling. "I can never write in coaches, you know. Far too bumpy."

Sarah agreed, then stretched out on her bed. Valerie went into her own smaller compartment and discreetly closed the curtain between them. Miss Gwinn took out her maple lap-desk and sorted her papers. The scratching of her crisp pen-tip was soon the only noise in the room.

Sarah slept. Only once did she stir, at the sound of Miss Gwinn rummaging for, and then lighting, a candle. The mid-afternoon light had dimmed considerably, and the rain assaulted them harder than ever.

A few hours later she opened her eyes to complete silence. With an effort, she raised herself and looked around. Miss Gwinn's candle had dwindled to a mere stump. Miss Gwinn herself was on the bed asleep. Her letter lay, half-finished, on the table where their suppers should have been waiting. Sarah was ravenous.

She went to the bowl of water on the bureau, now stone cold, and splashed her face and hands. "Miss Gwinn?" she whispered, venturing closer. She was about to shake her, but restrained herself upon recognizing the pale vacancy of pure exhaustion on the woman's lean face. She had flung her glasses on top of the letter. Sarah reached out to fold them up, and her gaze fell inevitably on what she'd written.

"My dearest Dorothy," she read, "I have now traveled for two days, with perhaps another six hours to go once we leave this unpleasant inn. My mother and Davie may not require my assistance at all by then, though my heart breaks to admit it. How I curse that pox to the lowest depths of . . ."

Here something was scratched out. Apparently Miss Gwinn had not been able to bring herself to commit such an indelicacy to paper. The contents took a more interesting turn, however. "My heart is also heavy with the thought of perhaps another month's separation from you. Already I feel a world away from our nightly fire, our tea which we drink in the rocking chairs, and your comforting laugh which makes all the day's trials seem nothing . . ."

She had not gone on. Either emotion or sleep had overcome her at this point and she had flung off her glasses and fallen onto her pillows. Sarah pulled away from the letter, discomfort clogging her throat. She looked at Miss Gwinn's closed eyes. Even when she saw her in this most vulnerable state, she found it difficult to imagine her experiencing, much less expressing so plaintively, such depths of empathy and longing. Sarah tried to imagine what Dorothy looked like, and wondered also what her own letters might sound like, were there such a friend in her life.

Such attachments, she knew, were hardly uncommon at girls' schools such as the one which employed these two women. Her own acquaintances still occasionally dissolved into the absurdities of pure infatuation whenever they recalled certain classmates or even instructors at their own institutions. Sarah's own youth had been impoverished on this account too. In this instance she could not follow Uncle Lionel's reasoning. Surely the likelihood of her following her mother's particular example would have been slim enough at such a place.

Her stomach lurched with hunger again. What had happened to their dinner? One of them ought to investigate, she decided, and without further ado, she walked down the stairs and straight into the tavern. The air was heavy with alcoholic stench and coarse laughter.

She felt again a warm rush of blood to her ears as the same gaggle of unwashed male faces turned to stare. An insulting murmur of comment ensued.

"Please." She cleared her throat and summoned what she hoped was an authoritative voice. "I'm looking for our landlord. Is he about, or perhaps his wife?"

No one made any attempt to answer her, but a rather short, balding man got to his feet clutching a pewter tankard. "Well then, byhap ye've been locked out of your room, luv? I daresay that should cause no problem. So 'appens I've an extra cot in mine . . . though I daresay neither of us'd want to be getting much sleep there."

Disgust and horror sent shivers through Sarah's body. She was about to duck back out of the room, all thoughts of supper quite forgotten, when another man, larger than the first and looking little more reputable, walked in and unwittingly blocked her escape. He stood, staring at her, and then at his friends, a slow-witted leer spreading on his face.

Sarah quickly considered her options. A scream might bring the landlord out from the kitchen, where he was obviously dallying in ignorance of the situation, but it might also inflame any number of these besotted louts to sudden and irrevocable violence. Reasoning with them was another possibility, though the glaze in nearly every pair of eyes bespoke little success.

"Let me through," she finally muttered through clenched teeth, preparing to push past him. "I'll trouble you no further."

"By the bones of good King George," the man behind her laughed, grabbing her wrist, "have you ever seen the like of this saucy wench?"

Sarah gasped as his rough hands closed around her wrists and shoved her hard against the wall. His face rushed down on her and his stale breath flared up her nostrils. She did scream — loudly, in fury. Somewhere behind her, the kitchen doors slammed open and feet scuffled on the hardwood floor. The jeers and shouts reached a deafening level, but still his body blocked her view, his left hand boldly swiping at her chest.

From the corner of her eye, she saw a flash of silver and heard a gurgled curse. The pressure on her wrist disappeared and she was stumbling forward, choking with shame, into someone else's grip. These hands were gentle, though, and set her back on her feet almost immediately.

She blinked up at a much younger man than the first, clad, to her surprise, in a fine footman's livery.

The laughter from the tables had changed tone now, and when she turned she saw her assailant leaning against a weathered post on which coats had been hung, clutching his ear and howling. Beside him, laughing with startling force, a richly dressed young woman in an emerald tailcoat and skirt stood brandishing a pewter tankard — the flash of silver, Sarah realized, had been its weight coming down upon his head. He was cursing her still, in language she could quite honestly say she had never heard the equal of before.

The woman raised the mug again, long auburn hair shining like a flame around her head as she did so. "Best remember, Gareth, the path of the flesh is the path to damnation." So saying, she flung the remainder of its contents onto his trousers.

The landlord, rubbing his hands together in a near panic, rushed to her. "Once again I must extend my deepest apologies, Lady Pym. I assure you I —"

"Rather a good thing I never take a meal myself without first inspecting the quarters it's prepared in. Nothing but the child's pride is injured, I trust?" Lady Pym, tugging the front of her coat straight, addressed the liveried servant, who nodded.

"It would appear not."

"I trust her bill will be reduced accordingly?"

"But of course, Lady Pym." The landlord nodded again, his jaw taut but his eyes miserable.

"Then I daresay we've all had enough drama for one evening. Theodore, find out where her room is and see that she gets back safely."

"Yes, my lady. Will it please you follow me, Miss?" Theodore indicated the stairway with a half-bow. Sarah nodded, and somewhat shakenly preceded him. As she mounted the first step, she glanced back at the still-smiling Lady Pym, who offered her a mock salute and waved her on her way.

CHAPTER 3

Sarah was awakened at what seemed a perfectly indecent hour, first by a heavy scraping along the bare floor just outside, and then the rude hammering of somebody's fist. Groggily, she sat up, the sheets tangled around her knees and her hair hanging into her face in a dark unkempt mess. Valerie staggered, blinking, into view.

"Yes, yes, all right." Sarah floundered for her dressing gown. Valerie, more efficient by virtue of her profession, proceeded to the door and opened it a crack. Sarah was grateful, having forgotten none of the details of her last incautious venture through the inn's corridors.

"It's your bath water, mum," a broad rural accent declared. "Now's the time we always bring it."

"Bath water?" Sarah raised her brows at Valerie, who shrugged. "I don't believe we've ordered any. Are you certain it's for this room?"

"Aye, we're sure." The voice was irritated, and the fist knocked again. "Beg your pardon, Miss, but me and Ginny've drug it all the way up here, me wiv a sore arm even, and we're not going to stand here all morning. Them friends of yours are keeping us busy enough."

"Perhaps it was Miss Gwinn." Sarah stood aside as Valerie unbolted the door. Two stocky girls pushed inside, tugging a huge metal can between them. A scented vapor rose from it, and Sarah had to admit that the prospect of a hot bath was more than appealing. Surely, even if Miss Gwinn had ordered the water, there would be enough to split between the three of them . . .

"Goes in there, I think." Ginny indicated Valerie's cubby-like chamber with a tilt of her chin. The two made off with the canister, bumping and scraping it across the floor. Miss Gwinn appeared, wrapping her dressing gown around herself. "Goodness," she murmured, observing the struggle with a raised brow.

Ginny emerged from the cubby, wiping damp hands on her apron. "We'll be up with the second can when ye're ready. I'll come back and check. For now we'd best be tending your fine friend up the hall." Again she gestured with her chin, and together with her companion plodded off down the hall.

Valerie, Sarah, and Miss Gwinn regarded each other in complete bafflement.

"But I never ordered anything," Miss Gwinn protested, when they attempted to pin the misunderstanding on her. "I certainly wouldn't have gone to the extra expense of . . ." she began, then caught herself, apparently recalling Sarah's more comfortable circumstances. Miss Gwinn's modesty, Sarah had already noted with admiration, did not preclude a certain scholarly pride she had no difficulty believing was quite justified.

"Shall I go and try to make some sense of it all, Miss?" Valerie asked.

"Yes, and why did they think we were connected with that party in the other wing?" Miss Gwinn asked. "I, for one, have never even met them!"

While they continued to debate, someone else knocked. When Sarah opened the door, half-expecting to see an unrequested trio of breakfast trays, she saw only a sealed envelope on a small china plate lying at the threshold.

"Perhaps it concerns our departure time," Miss Gwinn suggested.

Sarah read it aloud, her rising tone betraying her increasing surprise. " 'No doubt after last night's adventures you will doubly welcome the opportunity of a proper scalding. Our good landlord assures me that this service is provided quite out of the charity — and severe embarrassment — of his own character. I shall call upon you at half past nine, when I hope we shall be able to endure the inn's version of breakfast together. Yours respectfully, Lady Augusta J. Pym.' "

The two women stared at one another, saying

nothing. Finally, Miss Gwinn spoke. "Well, she seems a most valued patron here. And since you've the appointment with her, Miss Lindsay, perhaps you had better take the first portion of water."

Breakfast did indeed arrive forty minutes later, followed closely by Lady Pym herself. Sarah had found herself in some difficulty regarding her choice of a dress, but had finally settled on one of the better garments she had set aside for use in Bath, for company whose opinion she valued. The wide-sleeved organdy gown, high-necked for daytime wear, was pearl-gray with tiny blue stripes running the length of it. The color, she felt, flattered her eyes while the hourglass waist did adequate justice to her trim middle. She selected also the new flat shoes with cross-bands her uncle had brought her from London the month before but which she had not yet found the opportunity to wear.

When she rose to invite Lady Pym into her room, she was glad to have taken the trouble to adorn herself, despite the incongruity of the setting, for Lady Pym herself had apparently done no less. Also freshly scrubbed, she had donned a full-skirted garment resembling a riding costume adapted for indoor use and decorated with an embroidered collar and cuffs. Her hair was arranged in a rather daring asymmetrical configuration with a series of tiny ringlets framing her face. Miss Gwinn, of course, had relied upon the somberly dyed indoor costume befitting her profession, and beside Lady Pym's imposing figure Sarah felt scarcely more fashionable herself. Still, she grasped Lady Pym's hand and was relieved to find genuine friendliness, rather than the expected condescension, in her eyes.

"I see I have, fortunately, less advantage over you this morning than when we last met, Miss Lindsay," Lady Pym said, releasing Sarah's fingers after a robust squeeze. She then turned to Miss Gwinn. "I trust these unfortunate surroundings have not irretrievably dampened your spirits, either, for I look forward to considerably better breakfast conversation than I have enjoyed for some weeks."

"We are attempting to acclimate ourselves," Miss Gwinn assured her. Sarah noticed that Lady Pym had brought along one of her own maids, who whisked Valerie off to another breakfast room laid especially for servants.

"She'll prefer it," Lady Pym announced, taking a place on the inadequate settle Sarah and Miss Gwinn had moved from the corner. They made do with straight-backed chairs, one of which wobbled when Sarah brushed her skirts decorously flat on her lap. "Besides, I'm willing to pour my own tea in exchange for a little privacy."

"Quite so." Miss Gwinn nodded in approval. "At the school we sometimes have the younger girls do it. The gossip that circles the dormitory the following afternoon is little less than unbelievable."

"Poor little minds, stuffed with sawdust when they arrive, no doubt. Takes a bit of doing to shake the last of it out." Lady Pym laughed, leaning her arm over the back of the settle. Sarah noted the contrast between the dark red satin of her tapered sleeve, perfectly matching the highlights of her hair, and the faded pattern on the upholstery. Lady Pym's face, too, seemed more fleshily real than it had in her hazy remembrances of the previous evening's ruckus. Her laughter was light and unquestionably feminine, in a special and vibrant sense. No doubt, Sarah reflected, her own malignancy had been partially responsible for her initially perceiving it as vengeful and harsh. Now, discoursing on the pettiness of small girls, her own nieces apparently rendering her something of an authority, Lady Pym managed to provoke even Miss Gwinn to smiles and finally a stifled titter. Breakfast passed pleasantly and somehow too quickly.

Staring at her third cup of tea, lukewarm by then, Lady Pym pursed her lips in thought. "On the whole, I think it's fairly fortunate I decided to have a look at that fly-pit they call the kitchen last night. Usually I never encounter anyone at these places. The disadvantage of reserving an entire floor for myself, but I've certainly taken my lessons there before!" Stretching out her long fingers, she was just able to brush aside the curtain and glance out at the courtyard. "The mud's let up a bit, I see. Rolling out this afternoon, are you?"

"As soon as the roads are passable, I expect," Sarah said.

"It was the mud, I presume, which forced you to this haven yourself?" Miss Gwinn ventured.

"Oh, yes, certainly. In fact, I'm but an hour's ride from my property now. I pushed my people to hurry on, but you know how fate can be. I've been to the Midlands, you know — a sick sister, who recovered quite rapidly when I wrote her a note for some unpleasant gambling debts she'd run up with two gentlemen at her last fête. We live and learn."

43

"I myself am going to Bath to attend a sickbed." Miss Gwinn stared at the saucer and cup on her lap. Sarah, observing her renewed distress, felt pangs of guilt about going on a mere holiday herself, and somehow it seemed appropriate that she should confess this.

"Oh, but I'd assumed you were traveling together." Lady Pym looked at them with interest. "You seem like the oldest of friends."

"No doubt any stranger would assume the same of the three of us, were he to observe us here laughing." Sarah smiled modestly.

"Listen, perhaps I could persuade you both to forfeit your coach passages and come as my guests instead. Certainly I can offer Miss Lindsay more hospitality than Bath can, these days, and Miss Gwinn could resume her own journey within the week, if needs be."

"A very kind offer." Miss Gwinn looked up quickly, almost alarmed. "But my family situation precludes my acceptance. In such circumstances time is very valuable to me. I do beg your understanding, Lady Pym."

"But of course! I'd no idea your mission was so grave."

"I . . . should not have willingly left my school otherwise." Miss Gwinn stared at her lap again, her voice betraying a note of strain. Sarah recalled the letter she had so inconsiderately perused, and felt her skin burn.

"But you, Miss Lindsay?" Lady Pym, not allowing for an uncomfortable silence to develop, swung about on the settle to face Sarah squarely.

44

"Well . . . I should feel unhappy to desert Miss Gwinn, now that we've become friends."

"Nonsense," Miss Gwinn said through taut lips. A thin crease flickered on her forehead, then vanished as if she had forced it away in a supreme effort to avoid attracting any further attention to herself. Pity, Sarah sensed, was what she resented most. "Of course you must go if you wish, Miss Lindsay. It isn't much further at all, and it's unlikely we would see much of one another at Bath anyhow. Of course she'll accept, Lady Pym."

"Well, then, we're settled! Miss Lindsay will come with me this afternoon, and Miss Gwinn will call on me as soon as time permits. My offer of shelter will stand."

"I thank you."

"And I, of course," Sarah nodded. For the first time, her journey began to inspire in her a sense of enthusiasm, and not merely dread and the need to flee further, further from her shame.

"In fact, I shall send a member of my own company with you in Miss Lindsay's stead, Miss Gwinn. Millicent has had experience nursing. She will assist you in any way possible, and I shall provide her with return fare when you tire of her."

"I couldn't possibly accept such generosity."

"You mean charity, and this isn't. Miss Lindsay's fare is paid, anyhow, and we can't upset our coachman's ledgers. I have enough grief with my own. Let me settle it with them."

Lady Pym stood, slapping her knees with resolution as she did so. Sarah stared, suddenly feeling quite plain and inadequate by comparison.

Lady Pym was the color of fire, and Sarah herself suggested nothing so much as a pool of day-old tea.

"I'll return shortly," Lady Pym announced, and sailed out again.

Within the hour, the arrangements were indeed complete. They stood in the courtyard, amid fantastic mud puddles and cases. Sarah pressed Lady Gwinn's hands in her own. The young man in blue gestured from the coach window.

"Deserting us, Miss Lindsay! I've a good mind not to forgive you!"

"Oh, I couldn't bear that." Sarah smiled, embarrassed that Lady Pym looked amused also. The bulky Millicent stormed up the steps, one large travel-case in each hand.

"I'll write," Miss Gwinn promised, offering a more formal handshake to Lady Pym. "I thank you again."

"Unnecessary," Lady Pym asserted. Presently the carriage churned out of the courtyard, its wheels throwing up showers of brown water. Lady Pym's private coach rolled straight into the space it had vacated. It was much smaller than the first, designed of course to hold fewer passengers, but was finely upholstered and had been wiped clean of mud. The servants waited in a separate carriage behind them. Theodore, the impeccably liveried gentleman Sarah recalled from the tavern fracas, offered a hand up. Lady Pym accepted the boost, laughing. They settled themselves in good spirits. Lady Pym unwrapped a small loaf of bread, still warm, from a white cloth fastened with a royal blue thread.

"A parting gift from our landlord," she explained, and unwrapped a pearl-handled knife as well.

CHAPTER 4

Sarah had noticed the countryside changing even before Lady Pym, leaning back in her seat, announced that they had entered the outskirts of her own grounds. "You'll find Pym House isolated, but pleasantly so. I have never found solitude a problem myself."

"I see." Sarah couldn't tell whether this meant that Augusta Pym courted solitude, as Uncle Lionel was said to, or whether she harbored a multitude of friends who called as often as she wished. Feeling it would be impolite to quibble, she let the matter rest and diverted her attention back outside.

She tried to define, as she watched the lazy animals plodding between the low stone fences and biting at the craggy trees, exactly what about Lady Pym's pastures conveyed to her such a sense of completeness. Certainly countless other, similar views, had failed to stir in her anything but a vague aesthetic pleasure which might affect any village-dweller unused to extreme rusticity. She smiled at the checkerboard patterns of yellow and green fields, the sculpted serenity of each scattered cottage, all aglow from the spring showers. The torrents of mud had not reached this far uphill, either.

Lady Pym, reading her thoughts, peeled off her gloves. "The spring has been kind to us this year. My neighbors, the Gerards, were less fortunate. A good portion of their private garden was completely washed away last month. Isabel had just hired someone to arrange it for her, and was in quite a pet over it, I can tell you. You'll meet her almost immediately. She has her servants watch my house, I think, so she can trot over the moment I return from anywhere."

"Is she a very close friend of yours, then?"

"Oh, yes. When I was first widowed, I couldn't have managed without her. Not grief, you understand, though there was that, but the crushing weight of the practical."

"I had wondered whether you had a husband living. It seemed indelicate to ask."

"Really? Why?" Lady Pym seemed surprised. "Ah,

well, we may as well clear it up now, though. My husband was Sir Lewis Pym, a baronet's son. He died three years ago of pneumonia. His title will die out now, since we were childless."

"Oh. I'm sorry."

"People always say that. Actually, it caused no friction whatever between us."

They were drawing closer to the house, for Sarah began to see colorful patches of flowers, and large clusters of trees. The willows placed along the roadside dipped and bowed as the horses cantered past, as if paying homage to their mistress's return.

"My husband's grandfather had this path cut specially, feeling the view of the house was the best from this incline. He allowed the more convenient route to completely disintegrate. I never saw the old fellow's wisdom until I was coming over the hill from a party at midnight, and the moon was right over the front turret." She pointed to the top of the house, just visible. "I made the coach stop and I stared for a full half an hour. Rumors flew about that I'd gone daft for some time after."

"I can imagine."

"What, that I'm daft?"

Sarah blushed. Pym House was, she saw, a house designed in the wake of the Gothic Revival, which had enjoyed much popularity the previous century. A carved façade of silvery stone lay wedged behind four spherical towers which had been topped with medieval-style French battlements. Moon-shaped windows scored the mottled shafts. A sloping lawn, tastefully sprinkled with trees and short shrubs, crawled down the incline to be stopped by a short, gated wall. A painted carving, bearing a family crest held aloft by white cherubs, glittered with raindrops over double front doors.

"Our really special gardens are in the back," Lady Pym said. "I'll have the tea things brought out there as soon as you've been shown to your room. The tower one is magnificent, though some of my guests say the round walls make them ill. And you'll be happy to know we have no ghosts or torture chambers. We were built too late for that sort of thing, appearances to the contrary."

The servants' carriage rolled up behind them. Sarah soon found herself submerged in a mass exodus of bodies and luggage. She watched Valerie, supervising the unloading of their own things, with relief.

"My housekeeper will take charge of you for the moment." Lady Pym brought up an angular woman who seemed surprisingly young for so important an office. "This is Madame Lothaire."

"Miss Lindsay, welcome." The extremely composed woman inclined her head slightly.

Lady Pym explained her idea to have tea in the garden, resting her hand on Lothaire's black-sleeved arm as she spoke. With a veiled smile, Lothaire watched Lady Pym move off and then asked if Sarah would follow her. She nodded, and obeyed. Madame Lothaire, lips together, efficiently disentangled her from the melée and ushered her up a wide staircase laid with a Turkish carpet, then to a range of bedrooms facing west.

"You may have your choice of any of these, including the tower room, Lady Pym says. I shall show you each and then you may decide. If at any time you wish to change, you need only inform one of us before lunch, and your things will be removed in the afternoon. After that time I'm afraid our various duties would preclude such promptness."

"I . . . understand." Sarah was rather dazzled by such blunt efficiency. Only now, in the steadier light of the hallway, did she detect a few gray hairs embedded in Madame Lothaire's sensible hazel-colored knot, and a vague hint of strain around the pupils of her eyes that belied Sarah's earlier impression of relative youth. Nodding, Madame Lothaire led Sarah to the tower room and pushed open the low door to reveal a perfectly circular chamber; a charming grated window and a variety of medieval-style tapestries adorned the walls. The bed was a big four-poster with curtains. "Lady Pym calls this the Bayeux Room. She had most of these tapestries specially made."

"They're very fine."

"If you do take this room, you must exercise great caution in the placing of your candles. When Mrs. Gerard stayed here prior to her marriage she accidentally singed the corner of that one next to the bed. Lady Pym was most upset with her."

Sarah was surprised to notice a slight tugging at the corners of Madame's lips, as if she were trying to suppress a smile of amusement. No doubt any argument involving Lady Pym would indeed be quite volatile and even embarrassing in retrospect.

"I'm really very pleased with this room, Madame Lothaire, and I promise to be careful. Will you have my things sent up immediately? I should like to wash and change for tea."

Madame Lothaire tipped her head in compliance.

"I'll see to it, ma'am. Lady Pym will send for you when tea is ready. Meantime I'll leave you to settle in. The bell-pull is just there, near the bedpost. You will use it, of course, should you require anything."

"Of course. Thank you, Madame Lothaire."

"Yes, ma'am." Lothaire departed, leaving Sarah to sink onto the bed in welcome privacy. Miss Gwinn and the rest of the coach passengers were due at Bath in another hour or so, she decided. She attempted, guiltlessly, to imagine the shock on the face of Mrs. Waterbury, her arranged hostess, when she received the message forwarded to her via Lady Pym's servant Margaret. She would, of course, dispatch a second message to Uncle Lionel posthaste and possibly one to Pym House as well. The impromptu, almost daring nature of her detour afforded her several minutes of private delight, sufficient to temporarily erase the bitterness and pain which had necessitated her flight in the first place. The relief was indeed sweet balm.

Someone knocked at her door. Hastily, she stood and composed herself. Her visitor proved to be Valerie, and a pair of male servants bearing the trunk. A basin and a pitcher of warm water arrived moments later, with a message that she was to join Lady Pym in the garden as soon as she felt adequately refreshed.

In a flurry of excitement, Valerie helped her change and rearrange her hair. "They've given me a room just underneath yours, Miss, so if you were to need me I'd never be more than a heartbeat away. It's a very nice room, too, looking out at the garden and with a very nice lacy curtain . . ."

"Lady Pym's servants live well, it appears."

"Oh yes, ma'am, and one of the girls was telling me in the carriage that people send their daughters from twenty miles away to look for positions with Lady Pym because she's so kind to them, and pays so well. She takes on as many as she can, within reason, but never anyone who's slovenly or stupid, this girl said. Mind, that might have been just to puff herself up a bit."

"Perhaps so," Sarah laughed. "There, thank you, Valerie, I'll be going down now. Will you find out the way to the garden? If I got lost in here I might never be recovered!"

"No fear of that, Miss," Valerie bubbled, and disappeared. Soon Sarah found herself being escorted by another young maid down the stairs, to another long hallway on the ground floor, and out into the private rear garden that Lady Pym had, justifiably, referred to with such pride. A small table was laden with cakes and a silver tea setting; Lady Pym, dressed in a light blue riding outfit and a matching broad-brimmed hat, gestured to her.

"I always plan a late dinner because my cook's teas are so irresistible," she said, choosing a sweet.

Thanking her, Sarah did the same. "Your staff seems extraordinarily capable. Our own can hardly compare, I must admit. But then, my uncle takes little interest in tea except when he's expecting clients or lawyers."

"A crying shame. In some ways, tea is the day's most important meal. Gives the mind a rest and the stomach a boost. Your uncle is a businessman, then?"

"Yes." Sarah almost hated to admit this, since it was clear that Lady Pym belonged to a higher class, one that could afford to remain vocationally idle thanks to the support of various estates and investments. If Lady Pym was struck by their social inequality, however, she was too polished to reveal it.

"My late husband fancied himself a musical composer," she declared instead. "He was entirely unconcerned by the fact that nature had spared him no talent whatsoever. He'd make us listen to his new arrangements after every dinner party. Excruciating! We were hard pressed to find guests after a while."

"If it gave him pleasure, surely that was what mattered?"

"Oh, you needn't be so subtle. I'm not consumed with grief each time I speak of him. I know he'd prefer to be remembered with humor. He was a man of high spirits himself."

"You were well-suited, then."

"Yes, we were. We arranged our own marriage, in fact. It was no love match, but in time we were beloved friends, more than even we expected."

"I'm glad." The laughter the two had shared no doubt accounted for that, Sarah decided, and found it totally impossible to imagine herself ever sharing laughter, save possibly that of a most sadistic nature, with Mr. Hyde.

"You are not musical?"

"Not especially."

"What are you, then? How do you describe yourself, in the way that Sir Lewis called himself a composer?"

"Why, I say nothing, of course! Aside from

spinster. I'll be using that word more frequently as I grow older, too."

"And does that word please you?"

"In a way, it's a comfort."

"Well, that's interesting. But do choose something more flattering. What profession would suit you?"

"If I were a man, you mean?" This question was puzzling. Certainly it had never been addressed to her before in the company of ladies. Did Lady Pym suppose she was that close to the working class? She stammered something noncommittal, but Lady Pym would not be placated.

"This is my garden, Miss Lindsay, and therefore you must play by my rules. Answer."

"Well . . . I suppose I would say a banker. When I was small I often watched my uncle and his associates at work. I heard a great deal about monetary matters and the settling of accounts. I suppose I was always disposed to take an interest in such things. Had I been his nephew I should of course have been sent to work for him long ago."

"Yes, perfectly ridiculous, isn't it? A perfectly dense boy would get employed without question, while a far more capable woman is simply brushed aside into the marriage pool. In some ways our modern world is barbaric."

"I doubt many women would want to change it."

"I don't deny there's ignorance within our sex. We ought to divide people more accurately, though, for instance into the capable and the non-capable and not merely into the male and the not-male."

Sarah shrugged. She had no intention of discussing politics at tea, which was usually considered a terrible breach of etiquette. "Perhaps you're right."

"Of course I'm right. It's only common sense. Anyhow, banking is certainly not what I thought you would say. I was half-expecting poet or artist."

This did startle Sarah. She thought of Lord Byron again, wailing in his metal leg-brace. "But why? Do I seem dreamy and abstracted to you?" She had seen few poets in person, but everybody knew this was how they behaved. Only the most socially secure hostesses dared to display them. One never knew what they might say or do.

"I don't know. In a sense, you do."

"I assure you —" Sarah's cheeks flushed deeply, and she fumbled to put down her teacup. "I have scarcely had the experiences and . . . I must say, the excesses which foster a poetic temperament. The only volumes I would even dare put a pen to would be the household ledgers I will one day be forced to tend."

"Well, then, this evening I'll show you my own estate volumes. They're in a terrible state through little fault of my own. You can advise me."

"With all respect, Lady Pym, I am hardly qualified to do that!"

"I'm sure in whatever ventures you turn to you are immoderately successful."

The arrival of the same maid who had conducted Sarah downstairs made a reply thankfully unnecessary. "Mrs. Gerard is here, madam."

"As I expected." Lady Pym settled back, smiling. "Yes, I'll see her."

Sarah looked forward to seeing at last the bold

woman who had set fire to the tower room and sent her servants to spy on her neighbor.

Moments later a beautiful and intriguing creature swept into the garden. Her hair and skin tone were as light as gold, and Lady Pym's expression softened noticeably when the young woman flung herself into a seat between them and reached for some cake. "God's blood, Augusta, you always return from these jaunts looking disgustingly rested! I have to spend a full week in bed when I do — the dust, the noise, and all that mud!" She leaned over to kiss Lady Pym's temple, then turned on Sarah, brazenly curious. "Found yourself a new admirer, too. I swear, my fox."

Lady Pym introduced Sarah. She did not get the chance to repeat Mrs. Gerard's name.

"Oh, you know who I am already," Mrs. Gerard interrupted. "Of course you'll come to my house for tea tomorrow. I won't invite you, Augusta, because you know your solicitors are coming."

"As usual, you know my own schedule better than I. You're welcome to Miss Lindsay for the afternoon, but you must have her back before dinner. Stay yourself, if you like."

"Nonsense, I'm a married woman now. I have my duties at home, bossy Augusta. Invite my husband and me to a proper dinner party again, and I may change my mind. Not until."

"It will take me some time to have the invitations drawn up. Word-of-mouth would never do for a household of your caliber."

"True. Now, have you shown Miss Lindsay your famous salon? Half the volumes are dedicated to your rude hostess, you know, Miss Lindsay. She has a picture of everyone who ever entered there."

"Not a few were really dedicated to Lewis, my dear. Don't forget."

"Oh, Lewis, good heavens, what does that matter? No one with sense credited that salon to anyone but you. Dear Miss Lindsay, don't be alarmed, but I might as well tell you outright that I have no respect for men. Especially not my husband, as evidenced by the fact that I accepted his hand at all. Your new friend hasn't either, though she's loathe to admit it. I take it you're not engaged yet? Well, there's a relief, though you may as well get it over with one of these days. Things get much easier after one gives up all silly expectations. We'll discuss it tomorrow, no doubt. Now, dear, on your travels did you hear about poor King Willy, taking another turn with his poor withered lungs? We'll have a Queen within the year, I warrant you, and that night I'll be throwing a ball, believe me. You'll come, I needn't add."

"Oh, please, Isabel, do stop your mouth with some tea! It's quite likely to rust as it is." Laughing, Lady Pym pushed a cup toward her.

Sarah began to feel left out of the dizzying barrage of conversation that ensued, lightning fast, between the two for nearly an hour. At last, to her relief, Mrs. Gerard wandered off to her carriage, Lady Pym pretending to hurl a tea-cake after her. Screaming with laughter, Mrs. Gerard actually picked up her skirts and loped most indecorously back into the house. Sarah stared, dumbstruck, never dreaming such relaxed banter and tomfoolery could exist between any friends who had passed school age. She watched Lady Pym leaning back in her chair, laughing so hard it seemed the buttons on her jacket would spring off, and experienced a puzzling surge of regret and sorrow that no one had ever attempted to toss even a small biscuit after her.

"You'll have quite a time tomorrow," her hostess warned, to which Sarah could only nod with some trepidation.

After dinner, Lady Pym led her to the fabled salon, which turned out to be a richly furnished sitting room at the rear of the house, the walls lined with bookcases and crammed with a variety of portraits, silhouettes, and miniatures depicting numerous men and women of varying ages and attractiveness, though each painted or sketched face bore the unmistakable stamp of intelligence and forceful personality. Clearly, Lady Pym chose her intimate circle with care and taste.

"We would meet in here twice a week," she explained, "and would read to one another, argue, or simply laugh together for hours on end. Many of our guests would stay the night, and we would stroll the grounds by moonlight, reciting and composing until we fell asleep, exhausted. Each member of the salon was required to produce a picture to hang in the room, and to donate any volume having particular significance to the group." She indicated first the walls, then the bookshelf.

"And does the group no longer meet?"

"We continued to, for approximately a year and a half after Lewis's death. Then I went abroad for six months, and many of the other members scattered, too. We each took away something very inspiring and lasting, I think, and felt it better to preserve those memories intact than to try to recreate even one of them. In time, we may begin to gather here again . . . who can say?"

"Mrs. Gerard was a member, I see." Sarah touched the frame of the small oil painting just over the fireplace, which featured Isabel Gerard's smiling face, angled coyly over a partially bared shoulder, the minute detail of her strong white teeth poking from beneath a sensuous lip. "The artist captured her very well."

"She was Miss Finch then — in fact, she and Mr. Gerard met here, at a house party just before Lewis's death. He was not involved in our circle, however." While Sarah studied the portrait and others beside, above, and below it, Lady Pym seated herself at the corner piano and plucked out a few notes. "Do you play, Miss Lindsay?"

"My governess taught me the rudiments . . . years ago."

She laughed. "As did mine before her. Here, let me play you something of my husband's — then you'll believe my stories of his utter incompetence at the instrument." She did so, playing herself with no great expertise, but with good spirit. The composition was duly wretched, tedious in parts and exceptionally cacophonous in others. She stopped when Sarah winced, and laced her fingers under her chin. "That was intended to be a ballet, which we may be thankful he abandoned early on. But come here, now you try something."

They picked out tunes, again with no degree of

expertise but with enjoyment, for what Sarah estimated was close to an hour. Finally, Sarah took her fingers from the keys and faced her hostess. "I do so like Pym House. I thank you again for inviting me."

Lady Pym regarded her guest kindly, and Sarah decided she was genuinely flattered. "Tomorrow, those ledgers," Lady Pym promised. "Now perhaps we had better retire."

The time was, in fact, later than Sarah had supposed. Still, she was restless and overstimulated by the startling variety of what had taken place since the morning. She requested, therefore, a book to take to her room.

"But of course. We have plenty, as you can see."

"May I, then . . ." Sarah stood and made a tentative path for the nearest shelf. To her surprise, Lady Pym rose too, smoothly stepped in front of her, and diverted her to a different case.

"Oh, I don't think anything in that collection will interest you," she said hastily. "Merely some boring scientific works my husband collected. No doubt some of these would be more to your taste — current novels, poetry, general essays perhaps."

"Well . . . yes, thank you." After making a hasty and rather self-conscious perusal, Sarah chose something she was not really interested in and made a demure retreat. Lady Pym likewise disappeared to make her own preparations for bed.

"I have a very full day planned for tomorrow," she warned cheerfully, turning down the hall.

Servants appeared to attend to each of them, seemingly without signals of any kind. Sarah again wondered at this efficient, tightly controlled household, and the extraordinary personality of Lady Pym which permeated every room.

In bed, some time later, Sarah found that the volume she had chosen, one of Mrs. Radcliffe's later works, was little to her taste. She pushed it aside, and stared at the ceiling. Unfamiliar rooms always unsettled her. She eyed the dim patterns of the tapestries, which consisted largely of unicorns and crusaders and were barely visible in the fluttering candlelight. Sleep eluded her as surely as literary involvement had before. She ought to have chosen more than one book. There had been plenty of others downstairs . . .

Her hand strayed to the bell-pull, then stopped. Valerie would scarcely be able to choose another one for her, nor in all likelihood could she find the salon in the dark. If one of Lady Pym's own servants discovered her wandering through the house on such a vague mission, an unpleasant misunderstanding could result.

Sarah could see only one course of action. Mindful of the tapestries, she took up her candle and her dressing gown and padded downstairs. The door of the salon shimmered as she approached it, and was slightly ajar.

She slid inside, brushing her hand along the side of the piano to guide herself in the near-darkness. She used her candle to light others nearer the bookshelves. After returning the Radcliffe, she scanned the titles for something more suitable. She recalled Lady Pym's panic when she had approached the glass case, a reaction that seemed inappropriate to a stack of tepid scientific treatises.

It was this case she picked her way back to. She

peered through the glass, squinting. A number of the titles were French, but did not seem particularly scientific. Some merely bore a single title, presumably a character's name, for the most part feminine. Scowling, she touched the latch and found it steadfast. Her hand fell away when she perceived a muffled noise behind her. Heart thudding, she turned to see no one.

Relief and exhaustion swept over her in a warm wave. The time had come for sleep, she knew. Careful to leave the salon just as she had found it, she retreated upstairs and tunneled under the bedclothes. In the moment before sleep, an unusual image flashed through her mind: a smiling fox, scurrying through a tangle of rosebushes. It made little sense to her until she recalled Isabel's teasing name for her friend Augusta: "my fox."

CHAPTER 5

The sun gushed through the half-open curtains and onto her pillows warm and golden. Sarah's eyes opened to an almost continuous splash of daylight which spun along the round walls and furniture. It drew the tapestry figures into bold relief — and, she thought at first, animation. From the window came the faint titter of birdsong, and loud women's laughter. One of the laughs was certainly Lady Pym's.

Sarah rose and shoved the curtain further to one side. Lady Pym was indeed below in the yard. The sunlight flashed off her brightly colored field clothing and her broad-brimmed hat. She was holding an immense bow, and was skipping between heaps of long arrows piled up on the grass. Beside her stood a tall woman, similarly dressed, but the silvery-white braid of hair on her shoulder proclaimed her to be much older. She, too, held a bow, and was just fitting an arrow into it. Lady Pym boisterously challenged her. Two targets had been set up further down the lawn, and several missile-shafts already protruded from the canvas. Clearly, the contest had been going on for some time.

Lady Pym's new guest was a good shot. Her next arrow arched, tail feathers glinting, to join the others near the center of the painted circle. Yet Lady Pym was hardly inadequate herself, and on the whole the two seemed well-matched.

Well-matched . . . Sarah's heart gave a self-conscious lurch. She was, she remembered sharply, a very new addition to her hostess's well-bred, not to mention well-read, coterie. Observing Lady Pym at ease with this sophisticated friend made her feel as though one of those slim arrows had veered wildly off course and penetrated the front of her dressing gown. Perhaps they were discussing her even now, Pym spinning the older woman a humorous and patronizing tale to explain the advent of her latest pet: "Yes, dear, and she's so refreshingly simple! Isabel concurs with me. That sort of naive prattle is just what we'd hoped for. Isn't Racine deadly after a while?"

This led, in turn, to less happy speculations. Perhaps the fairness of their archery contest was not testament to Lady Pym's skill, but rather to her cunning. There was little question now, as arrows rained from her bow, that she would prevail. Had her previous shots, just short of perfection, been only decoys, meant to distract the older woman, to give her an illusion of superiority?

Her last arrows spent, Lady Pym threw her bow to the ground and stood with her fists propped on her hips. Sarah saw clearly the red flush on her round cheeks, the glint of her white teeth. Her bested opponent stared at the target for some time. Then she marched over to administer an embrace, much as Mrs. Gerard had at tea. The two linked arms and strolled out of sight.

"Miss? Miss, are you awake? May I enter?"

Sarah jumped. Apparently the maid had been knocking for some time. She ran to the bolt.

"I'm not quite alert yet," she apologized, flustered, as the young woman carried in a jar of hot water for the basin. "Yes, please do bring that in."

"Tea will be ready downstairs shortly, unless you'd prefer yours up here."

"Well . . . perhaps I'd better. Lady Pym appears to have other guests."

"You mean Mrs. Lamb? Yes, she's one of madam's favorite friends. But I'm sure they wouldn't mind you interrupting them."

"Has Mrs. Lamb come from very far to visit?"

"Not really, Miss." The maid poured the water from pitcher to bowl, biting her lip in concentration. "She lives in the next village over, though she keeps rooms in London and Dover as well."

"I'm sure she does."

"Will Miss be taking tea downstairs or here?"

Sarah found herself suddenly wrapped in a very

black mood. The thought of Lady Pym romping downstairs with another, preferred guest rankled her. Irrational, she knew. What she ought to do was divert herself.

"I don't think I'll take tea at all just yet. But before you go, tell me something."

"Yes, Miss?"

"Which . . . which room was Sir Lewis's? Does Lady Pym still keep his things there?"

"Yes, Miss, though he hasn't been with us for some time."

"Does Lady Pym's room adjoin his?"

"Well, no, hers is one floor up."

"Thank you. I shall dress now. Send Valerie to me."

"Yes, Miss." The girl left obviously thinking her quite mad. Sarah washed quickly, undoing her hair in preparation for Valerie. When Valerie arrived, Sarah avoided the usual morning banter. "Valerie, you're going to help me do something. It's to be kept secret."

"Really, Miss? What is it?" Valerie was wide-eyed.

"I wish to see Lady Pym's late husband's room is all. I feel that, as long as we're to be guests here, we ought to know what sort of man he was, and to what degree . . . respectable."

"Very sensible, I'm sure, Miss. Have we . . . begging your pardon, Miss . . . any reason to suspect the contrary?"

"Not really, but a bit of prudence is never misplaced, don't you think? Come, finish lacing me up — there's no telling when lady Pym might send for me."

"Oh, yes, Miss." Valerie beamed with excitement.

They struck out a few moments later, proceeding down the empty hall with an excessive degree of caution. Sir Lewis's room was not locked — in fact, the door stood partially ajar, and Sarah slipped inside, leaving Valerie to stand guard by the entry.

The room was very still, too immaculate and undisturbed to suggest any lingering aura of Sir Lewis, or of the married Pyms as a couple. Rather, the composed manner of the objects, and the logical arrangement of his portrait and other remaining effects, suggested a small but indifferent museum. Lady Pym had been truthful, Sarah believed, when she had asserted that theirs had been no love match. Certainly no agony of remorse and loneliness had prompted her to retain any of his clothing or ornaments, for his wardrobe, also propped open, was empty, and the books she had expected to find had most likely been removed to the cases downstairs. A single tray of rings and cravat-pins stood in the center of the dresser, the tiny objects tangled together and long unadmired. Beside the tray stood a bronze statuette, in the Greek mode, of a young man hoisting a spear. In modesty she averted her eyes from this relic.

"Bit of a funny bird, wasn't he, Miss?" Valerie said, then looked sheepish when Sarah lifted her brows at her. "His picture, I mean. His face is soft somehow, not like I expected."

Sarah examined the portrait too, and saw a certain validity in this statement. Sir Lewis's bewhiskered jaw and spiky graying hair were masculine enough, and his tailored dark suit spoke of wealth and confidence. His eyes and mouth, however, betrayed a degree of sensuality unusual in a man. His stiff collar parted at the throat to reveal very soft pale skin. Possibly, she thought, the artist was a woman, for these details reminded her of a similar depiction of the poet Shelley. But no, his name was clearly carved in the frame just below Sir Lewis's left hand: "Painted this month of January, 1832, Upon my Honored Friend Sir Lewis Pym's Forty-Second birthday, by Mr. Quinlan Rutgers, AE. XXV."

"Mr. Rutgers was little older than myself when he did this," Sarah observed, surprised. She brushed her hand over the tray of jewelry, and picked up a watch-casing which no longer held any watch. Prying it open, she found a lock of hair tied with a green thread. The hair, coarse and brown, was not Lady Pym's. She dropped it with distaste.

"We'd better go," she said. Valerie, holding a silver hairbrush with Sir Lewis's initials on it, looked up. The two crept back into the hall. No one noticed them.

Isabel Gerard's coach arrived to fetch Sarah at two, only minutes after the two nondescript solicitors had entered the foyer. Lady Pym banished them to the study and promised to join them after she'd seen Sarah off.

"I'm not concerned that Isabel will get the better of you," she said, as Isabel's chubby footman guided Sarah into her seat, "but I do beg you to remain patient when she starts boasting."

"I will." Sarah smiled. She stared at Lady Pym's eyes and wished she were spending the afternoon with her instead.

"Well, I don't have to lecture you on composure. Tell me about it at dinner. Bring her back safely, Hansen."

"Yes, Lady Pym." Hansen took his place at the reins with a brief salute.

They lurched out of the drive. Sarah watched Lady Pym trot back up the steps and disappear behind her twin front doors. As they passed through the gates, Sarah's fingers grew clammy. Briefly she wished she had refused Isabel's hospitality, though wandering aimlessly through the house while Lady Pym conducted private estate business was less than appealing. Overpowering though Isabel was, Sarah was certain she could entertain to perfection.

The Gerards' house was neither as large nor as stylish as Lady Pym's. It lay on the other side of two fields and some woodland, and the carriage crossed a small stream before hitting the gravel path to the front terrace. Hansen escorted her as far as the bell-rope, not entering himself, then left her to wait in the foyer until a maid conducted her into the presence of Isabel and two gentlemen.

One man was well-fed and ruddy, with straw-colored hair. The other, much leaner, wore a boldly striped waistcoat and tiny round spectacles. The first, she was not surprised to learn, was Mrs. Gerard's brother, Roderick Finch, and the second her husband, Mr. Sylvan Gerard. They ushered her into the drawing room with great formality, and led her to a peach-colored sofa with a rounded back. The rest of the room was decorated in similar lightly shaded fabrics, in the Rococo style favored by those of her uncle's generation. A large mirror, framed by twisted gilt edging and held in place by a fat-bellied cherub in each corner, hung just opposite her seat. This caused her some temporary distress as she was forced to contemplate her own appearance, which she never failed to find unsatisfactory. Her nose was entirely too thin, in her opinion, her skin not transparent enough to be esteemed by English people of fashion. These deficiencies seemed particularly galling as the splendid Isabel Gerard came to sit next to her, an effortless smile playing across her delicate lips and full, exceedingly fair cheeks. Her brother, Mr. Finch, obviously unaccustomed to receiving callers, placed himself at her other hand, and at what she considered claustrophobic proximity.

"Do you find our home pleasant?" Isabel asked, smiling as if challenging Sarah to give some unconventional and perhaps even startling reply. Mr. Gerard, who had assumed a seat facing her, regarded her indulgently over the tops of his spectacles. His eyes seemed to her mud-colored and uninteresting, but she began to consider him by far the most sympathetic person in the room. The stripes in his waistcoat, she saw, were entwined with representations of tiny snakes which gracefully wound their way up his chest and under his lapels.

"Exceedingly so, I'm sure," Sarah replied with as little deference as she could manage without seeming actually rude. Isabel Gerard was not taken in by her superficiality.

"Oh, it's not much compared to Pym House, I'll grant you that," she declared with a little sweep of her hand that seemed to cause her husband enough pain that he winced. "Still, we must manage as best we can. We hardly do without anything, and must compensate for our architectural inferiority with stimulating company."

"Do so quite well, indeed." Roderick Finch nodded, twisting around in his seat as a maid entered with tea-cakes and butter. He scarcely waited until she set the heaping tray down before he attacked it with singular devotion, allowing him little time to contribute to the conversation.

"Augusta rescued Miss Lindsay from some horrible roadside inn," Isabel informed the men, taking a scone with considerably more finesse than her brother. "She had just managed to crawl there through a mud-storm after a dreadful coach accident. She was holed up there for days on end with almost no hope for salvation, miles away from her most casual acquaintance."

"Good heavens, how beastly!" Roderick flinched as he reached for the sugar.

"The situation was hardly so dire," Sarah said, embarrassed. As she explained the truth, she sensed their disappointment, and her honesty gained her a sharp glance of reproach from Isabel.

"Well, you ought to find Pym House a pleasant sanctuary in any event." Sylvan Gerard played with his long watch chain. "Augusta has done well to keep it up as she has, I mean being a widow and all. Her husband Sir Lewis was an acquaintance of mine in London, you know, before I settled here. It was through his kind intervention that I first encountered Mrs. Gerard."

"Lady Pym had mentioned something of the sort."

"Indeed. Sir Lewis had many important friends, a

good many of them intellectuals. You've seen the library? A good many of those volumes are dedicated to him, and there are not a few novels circulating about that have some minor character or another who bears a notable resemblance to him." Sylvan paused to cough, then plucked off his glasses and polished them with his monogrammed napkin. "Of course, as is the way with intellectuals and especially artists, we cannot expect them to remember their host with complete objectivity and fairness. However, Miss Lindsay, I must advise you that whatever unfortunate gossip you may have encountered, Sir Lewis was a fine man, only mortal of course like the rest of us, and despite his expected fallibility in that regard, I have never hesitated to affirm my regard for him in any company."

"Miss Lindsay would know little of such things, dear," Isabel cautioned. "Augusta never speaks of him unless asked, and she would not be eager to repeat the sort of crass rumor you are referring to. Miss Lindsay would simply close her ears to it in any case."

"Lady Pym had great regard for him herself, from what I could gather, at random of course," Sarah ventured, struck with irrational panic that all three were somehow aware of her surreptitious visit to the rear chamber of Pym House that morning.

"As did many other people." Isabel flashed an insinuating smile that Sarah, for no particular reason, found offensive. "Augusta is very fortunate she can afford to treat her servants so generously. Had they a mind to be vindictive, some unsavory tales might be circulating still, I daresay."

"Oh, what harm can it do for a man to be a bit of a rake?" Roderick Finch interrupted in a petulant tone, uncrossing his legs and stretching them out from the sofa. "We all come to an end soon enough, as poor Sir Lewis has demonstrated. God forbid I should be put to rest with as little life experience under my belt as some can claim." His eyes fixed his brother-in-law, but the implied accusation only caused Mr. Gerard to smile.

"My brother would love to scandalize us all, had he but the nerve." Isabel laughed loudly, to Roderick's apparent displeasure. "Appearances are, as you no doubt agree, Miss Lindsay, hardly a reliable gauge. Roderick looks as though he's scratched his name on a chair in every tavern, but in reality the only wenches he harries are those in our kitchens, when they're a bit late with his pudding."

"You are offending Miss Lindsay, my puppet." Mr. Gerard patted his wife's hand.

She ignored the gesture, and him, completely. "But of course she knows I love Augusta dearly," she asserted, waving her hand. "I've turned a blind eye from her oftener than many others would, and have. She's a fox, dear Miss Lindsay, an absolute fox."

"A most intelligent woman, to be sure." Roderick hunched his round shoulders, and averted his face as if in resentment. Sarah began to wish her interview had already come to an end.

"I heard in town this morning that His Majesty is ill again," Mr. Gerard offered, apparently noticing her discomfort. At least in him she sensed some normal human decency, and was grateful to discuss court politics for some time and in a degree of detail which did not interest either his wife or her brother.

74

"Only a month now till Little Drina has her majority. I wonder, will he last that long?"

"Imagine our country under a woman's hand," Roderick Finch moaned, stretching his legs out again.

"Oh, yes." Lady Pym nodded in complete sympathy, spearing some vegetables she claimed had been raised in her own garden. "Rod Finch is an intolerable bore. Isabel indulges him in everything. He's younger by three years or so, and never forgets that their parents committed him to her care. The money he spends . . ."

Sitting there that evening, at the opposite side of the wide table, Sarah began to stiffen from the shoulders down. Lady Pym, noticing, paused too.

"Sarah?" she asked with unexpected formality. "You look as though you're in abject misery. What did she say to you, the brute?"

"Forgive me, Lady Pym." Sarah heard her own voice issue breathily, strained. She put down her fork. She had been near tears longer than she had cared to acknowledge. "Mrs. Gerard spoke of you, too. You . . . and your husband."

"Did she? She was not complimentary, I presume."

"She . . . she . . . no."

"And you felt obligated to tell me, yet solicitous of my feelings. I do understand. But I'm not at all horrified. Isabel is a notorious gossip, more skilled in innuendo than anyone I know. But innuendo is where it ends with her. I've never known her to be actually slanderous, and she'd never try it with one of my own guests. So I feel secure in assuring you that whatever she said, she's probably said to my face more than once. She can't help herself, I sometimes think. As much as I care about her —"

"Lady Pym, please," Sarah forced herself to interrupt hoarsely. "I am truly sorry to say this. I appreciate what you've done for me this week. I admire your estate, and yourself, greatly. But today I realized how little I belong here. Wit, to me, should not be a tool to jab and cut with. Rather, it should be an embellishment to intelligent language, used to give conversational pleasure to those we respect, or love. It should make our speech beautiful, not merely clever, or posturing, at all others' expense. I am not clever myself, certainly not as you and Mrs. Gerard are. My aspirations, with regard to those I like to call friends, are much simpler. Please forgive my bluntness, I beg you, but I must speak. If I am to be merely an audience for all manner of verbal dexterity, for eloquence of a caste I shall not attain, I would prefer the humiliation of being sent on my way without further attentions. Otherwise, I shall become only empty inside . . . empty, as I am right now." The tears were flowing — she felt them, but refused to submit to her agony by attempting to wipe them away.

Lady Pym, who had seemed prepared to interrupt her more than once, stared in silent wonder. "By heaven, Miss Lindsay. I . . . had no idea."

"I am not your equal, Lady Pym. There is no estate called Lindsay House, no deer park built by my great-grandfather for his descendants, and my Uncle Lionel rides off to Salisbury every other morning to maintain the single home and garden he did receive from his father." She swallowed.

Lady Pym folded her embroidered napkin and tucked it under her full plate. "You mistake me very much," she said.

"I apologize, then." Sarah was ready to concede the battle. Her face and neck were already on fire. She started to turn away. Lady Pym's fingers on her cheek stopped her.

"It was never an audience I wanted in you. Not in the way you think."

"I believe you, of course. I had no right to speak so offensively. I must beg the excuse of the dinner wine."

"You were astute in one sense. Wit can become hollow. I was hollow for a long time myself. It was Isabel who made the difference then. She was bitter and loud, and she made it plain to me that I was the dearest thing in England to her. Who could reject such flattering devotion?"

"Not I, I'm certain." Sarah wished Lady Pym would let her slide away and out of the room. Such blatant discussion of private emotions horrified her. Why wasn't Lady Pym embarrassed, too?

"I didn't, and I'm still glad of that. But now that I'm older, and different . . . I see that I'm still empty, too, in some ways. I hadn't your wisdom when I had your years." Her hand, at last, dropped away. "Not that I'm so very ancient now!" She laughed.

Sarah slid from her seat with relief. "Please excuse me now." Tears were clinging to her lashes again.

Lady Pym nodded. "You are a valued friend here, Sarah," she said just as Sarah reached the threshold. "I do hope you'll stay."

The answer came of itself, startling even Sarah. "I'll stay."

The following day was wonderfully free both of formality and any reminders of the dreadful scene at the table. Augusta asked Angela Lamb over, and the three women passed the time riding, playing cards, and discussing the merits of foreign foods. Isabel's name was not mentioned, and Sarah was grateful for Lady Pym's sensitivity in ensuring this would be the case. Word games were also studiously avoided.

Sarah grew fond of Angela Lamb fairly quickly; even though she was past sixty, she did not instantly appropriate to herself the final say in every matter, and never once made any unfavorable comparisons between the modern world and that of her own youth. Instead, she asked Sarah about her own village and relatives and listened to her responses with genuine interest.

"Uncle Lionel would be scandalized to see how we're spoiling her," Augusta said.

I don't deserve it, Sarah thought. She smiled, as if to say, "Don't stop."

"It's only spoiling if the person doesn't appreciate

it," Angela said. "Miss Lindsay isn't the type. Not like that Miss Ducharme, that is."

Augusta shifted uncomfortably in her seat. "That was a very different thing, Angela."

"Was it? One never knows." Angela's steady gaze leapt from Augusta to Sarah. Sarah lifted a brow. "Well, time I was going. You know I'm expected at Sir Teddy Forbes' tonight."

"You'll dine with us next week, I hope."

"If you want me, of course. Goodbye, Miss Lindsay, dear. Do keep our Augusta honest. And don't let her challenge you at archery."

"I wouldn't consider it." Sarah smiled, though Angela's cryptic remarks still puzzled her. After she'd gone, she decided to inquire.

"Oh," Augusta waved her hand with forced nonchalance, "Miss Ducharme was just a dreadful little Londoner I entertained here for a while."

"She was an unpleasant guest, you mean?"

"She was nothing like you."

"I see."

"Now, my question is: do I dare take you in to supper again, or should I keep mine in the kitchen with Madame Lothaire?" Augusta's tone was so light, and her manner so buoyant as she hauled Sarah out of her chair by the wrists, that Sarah forgot to be humiliated.

She grinned. "I should very much like to dine with you."

"Well, then that's straight. But if I become offensive, you must certainly tell me."

"I promise, if you will do the same."

79

"I don't know why you consider yourself such a cretin. You could run rings around Rabelais."

"I should hope I'm not that crude!"

"Really? Pity." Augusta released her, and they walked in to dinner.

Rather than taking a place opposite her, Sarah sat very close to Augusta. As they passed various dishes and decanters, their hands brushed together more than once. Sarah found this sensation strangely comforting, and was even purposely clumsy on one occasion. Augusta looked suspicious, but said nothing.

"Shall we visit the garden, before we go upstairs?" she proposed instead.

Eager to prolong her most pleasurable day in months, Sarah agreed.

They strolled a few paces apart in the darkness. Sarah had been vaguely surprised when Augusta did not take her arm right away, but covered her disappointment by chatting about flowers and the importance of gardens.

"Uncle Lionel had one specially made," she explained. "He never goes there, though, unless he has callers."

"Do you?" Augusta asked, looking pointedly at her.

Sarah flushed. "I spend a good deal of my time there. I don't have many callers."

"I see."

"Lady Pym . . ." Taking a deep breath, Sarah stopped walking, reached out boldly, and took Augusta's striped sleeve in her right hand. Augusta hung back, though she did not pull away. In the shadows, Sarah could see her brows knitting.

"Yes?"

"I . . . I wanted to tell you that I hope we shall always be good friends."

Augusta gave a guarded smile. "I'm sure we shall be, Miss Lindsay."

Sarah's heart beat wildly, threatening to ram her ribcage all the way up her throat. Fire raced through her, but she couldn't believe it was that same evil fire of damnation she's heard about on countless Sunday afternoons, the fire she'd hid from under trembling blankets when her little feet couldn't yet reach the bedboard. Abruptly she snatched up Augusta's lean hand and kissed it, more than once, feverishly, until her teeth grazed the knuckles.

She let go suddenly. Lady Pym stood frozen, her mouth partially open, her forehead damp. Sarah met her gaze evenly, swallowing back the rush of panic she now felt.

"I . . . had better go in," she muttered, and fled. Augusta did not follow, but when Sarah looked back just before entering the house, she caught her watching intently.

The terrace door closed between them.

In the darkness of the tower room, a white-faced figure loomed close. Grinning teeth were exposed by emaciated lips, black eyes burned indecently. A clot of black, scented hair dangled over the bedclothes.

"Flesh of my flesh," sang the creature, "dearest daughter. How like me you are."

In the corner of the room, in the chair, Sir Lewis Pym pared his long nails with a small letter-opener.

Her mother left the bed and climbed onto his lap. One of his hands snaked up her back into that tangle of curls. The other hand wielded the letter-opener like a small dagger. He sawed off a long, foul lock and held it out towards Sarah, then grinned. The gold watch-case, open, swung from a chain around his neck.

"A testament to eternal devotion," he said.

CHAPTER 6

Angela Lamb returned late the following morning, bearing a square, sheeted panel which she yielded to Augusta with a flourish. This, apparently, had been the object of their archery contest two days earlier.

"Mind, Pym, I'd have given it to you anyway," she said, nudging Isabel, who had driven in with her. "Can't have the likes of that thing hanging about in my house."

Augusta undid the sheeting, and they all paused to admire a very fine Italian landscape, featuring a smattering of craggy trees, a crumbled Ionic column, and a cluster of figures in togas in the background.

"I'm for a stroll." Isabel stretched her arms in boredom. "Anyone with me?"

They moved into the garden, and decided to navigate first the circular path around the house, and then the orchards beyond. They strolled arm in arm and in pairs. Sarah had extended her own arm first, instinctively, to Augusta, but was strangely relieved when Isabel swooped between them and appropriated Sarah for herself. Augusta and Angela walked together, beginning to discuss in detail their painting. From the snatches of talk Sarah heard as she trailed behind the two, she discovered that Angela had won the picture from Augusta some months before, and Augusta had insisted on the rematch.

Isabel noticed her interest. "They traveled together in Italy," she explained, "and chose it together. When they returned, they couldn't decide who should keep it, so they devised this silly wagering game. This way Angela has it for three months, then Augusta. A very happy little fiction, I'm sure."

"So Mrs. Lamb lost to Augusta purposely?"

"She'd never admit it, but I imagine so."

Sarah reflected on her former ungracious judgment on the contest with regret. She changed the topic. "Has Mrs. Lamb a family?"

"Oh yes, a daughter and a son, though she's widowed now. Her son is at Cambridge — King's, I believe — and the daughter married some country

84

squire in West Riding. Obviously living beyond the pale of civilization does not affect her adversely."

"Some might say you and Lady Pym are isolated here."

"Well, only when we wish to be. Or prefer others to think so. Incidentally, my brother wished me to thank you for the lovely conversation we all had . . . not that I heard him say anything of significance, and I hadn't expected him to remember your name, where you were staying, or anything we talked about. Still, he wanted me to deliver the message, and I have."

They were interrupted by a shout from Mrs. Lamb, who had whirled around to face them. "My turn to walk with Miss Lindsay!" she announced, dropping Augusta's arm and sweeping Sarah aside. Isabel stared, then shrugged, but Sarah saw her long lashes flick irritably as she moved to join her hostess.

Angela Lamb patted Sarah's hand, remarking on Augusta's good judgment in keeping her guest fit. "Your cheeks look positively flushed. We admire that here, you know. None of these wispy consumptives dragging about these lawns."

They headed into the orchard, the fragrant boughs dipping down into their path. Twigs brushed their hats and tugged their hair. Augusta and Isabel walked far ahead, talking quietly.

"Lady Pym must love Mrs. Gerard very much," Sarah said, surprised at her own audacity, though Angela maintained her composure.

"I expect there is love between them, yes. Not as

85

it was, of course. That was Isabel's choice. We mortals ought not to define every kind of love, though. We ought to be happy enough they exist at all."

"Yes," Sarah said, watching them.

Several paces ahead, Isabel turned to Augusta. "Miss Lindsay is very intelligent," she bit the words off like an accusation.

"Very." Augusta admired the birds circling the orchard. She broke off a leafy twig and shredded it as they walked.

"Her family can't be too important. Certainly I've never heard of them."

"You have. You heard of them the day you met Miss Lindsay."

Isabel's eyes contracted in annoyance. Her gold curls glittered in the sun. The Golden Dragon, Augusta had once dubbed her, years ago. They'd been in the east field, which was no longer empty, lounging in each other's arms. Augusta remembered such moments more frequently now that the pain no longer stabbed. She no longer had any desire to return to them, either. She preferred, instead, to keep them as precious memorials to a happiness now asleep, closed away in shiny lockets kept forever near the heart. Like those bits of young men's hair, passionately collected by Lewis.

Isabel's sleeve strained against Augusta's as her pace slowed and Isabel's picked up. The Golden Dragon was herself a captive now, Augusta knew. She had chosen her own bonds. Prometheus, Augusta thought: the bringer of fire, now imprisoned in its lasting heat.

"You always were one to quibble," Isabel said. "Look, darling, shall we go back and have tea now? All this talking's made my mouth dry as dust."

"Small wonder, Isabel," Angela teased.

They sought shelter in the relative cool of the portrait-filled salon. Augusta left to order a refreshment tray, and while she was gone, Sarah asked Angela if the room contained a picture of Miss Ducharme.

Isabel's brows shot up. "I shouldn't think so," she answered for Angela. "She was too recent. Has Augusta really told you about her? Not very tactful."

Sarah thought it best to let the subject wane. They talked about paintings instead. Isabel stretched her legs out on the sofa and crossed her ankles. Angela wandered to the piano and stabbed at a few keys. Sarah sat near the locked bookcase, which she couldn't resist gazing at once again. The faded titles still did not suggest anything scientific to her, though she did not have the grammatical knowledge to interpret those written in Latin and German. It occurred to her finally that they might be rare editions which Lady Pym — perhaps even following some request of her late husband's — preferred that no one handle. Her representing them as uninteresting to Sarah must have been merely a display of tact. It was less tactful of Sarah to continue brooding about the matter. She resolved to discontinue her speculation.

Augusta entered the room, smiling at Angela's musical dalliance. "Why don't you play us something, dearest? One of your Italian things, perhaps. Angela is the only one of us with any true talent," she told Sarah.

"Angela ought to have been an Italian," Isabel said.

"Nonsense! I could never have stood the heat."

"Miss Lindsay speaks Italian, I suppose?" Isabel asked with apparent boredom.

"None at all, I fear. My governess favored the French tongue almost exclusively."

"Pity."

"Do sing some of the sad ones, Angela. Since none of us will understand the words, we won't become despairing. And anyway those are quite the prettiest."

Angela laughed, pulled up the bench, and launched into a ballad Sarah had not heard before. Her voice was not exactly sweet, as the content may have demanded, but it was powerful and plaintive, and Angela deployed it with a confidence that made its flaws secondary, if not completely insignificant. The song seemed to concern an unhappy young woman — this much Sarah could discern through her knowledge of French — and she thought it likely that the predicament involved a love spurned or ended. The melody reinforced the subject's unhappiness, repeating a few chosen melancholy strains several times with little alteration. Sarah glanced at Lady Pym who was quietly mouthing the words. For a moment, Sarah imagined the salon filled with Augusta's sparkling acquaintances, the faces from the portraits, the men as beautiful as the women in their fashionable tailcoats and cravats, their small rings glittering on hands that cupped brandy glasses. As in the present, Isabel and

Augusta gazed at each other at particularly affecting points in the ballad.

Sarah was aware of her own disappointment in the fact that she could never equal such people in matters of intellect and dress. The language of the song was not beyond them, nor the sentiments it expressed alien and fictional. All of these ghosts she had conjured herself were filled with love, she knew, and basked in admiration of other lovers with commensurate experience and understanding. Her own importance paled beside them.

Angela finished, and they offered her many compliments. "Perhaps the Petrarch now?" she asked Augusta. "*Di pensier in pensier, di monte in monte, Mi guida Amor . . .*"

"Well, your voice will be tired." Augusta shook her head, resting her chin on her palm as the tea tray arrived. Isabel took the opportunity to discuss a recent trip to London, and Angela left the piano to partake in the sweets. Isabel recalled a gathering she had attended in the city, to her ultimate chagrin, at the home of someone who had recently fallen out of fashion among her usual set there. She had been treated to a demonstration of a certain dance which her hostess had assured her was all the rage at the palace, for it had been imported by Princess Victoria's German cousins and now their future queen would dance nothing else.

"But here, there's no sense in my merely describing it to you! Come, Augusta, you shall be my Prince Ferdinand for the moment. You'll catch on quickly, I daresay, as always."

Angela returned to the piano and plucked out an obliging tune, to Isabel's specifications, and Isabel grasped Augusta's two hands and hauled her to her feet. They pranced around the room, Isabel explaining graceful but complicated steps that did seem more German than English. As predicted, Augusta caught on quickly, and soon the two were performing very prettily around the sofa. Angela shouted her approval as she played.

Eventually, Augusta slowed, and wiped her temple. "Very invigorating, to be sure. The Princess must be fitter than we all supposed."

"Not I," said Angela firmly. "She's a sturdy sprout. She certainly handled herself well enough with that Sir John Conroy, when he supposed the pox had left her pliant."

"It was the typhus, dearest," Isabel corrected.

"I shall be glad enough to see England under a woman's aegis, myself," Augusta said, "though of course we mustn't rejoice to see His Majesty failing."

"Not our fault he was born with weak lungs," Isabel rationalized.

"Come, Sarah, your turn." To Sarah's surprise, Augusta whipped around and pulled her to her feet. "Surely you are a quick study, too."

"I should astonish myself if I were," Sarah mumbled. Augusta stood very close, warm breath on Sarah's forehead. One steady arm snaked around her waist; fine long fingers locked through Sarah's. Sarah's mouth went dry suddenly, as she recalled the kisses she had imprudently bestowed the night before, and her pulse quickened as Lady Pym's strong arms turned her across the room. Angela, laughing as she played the piano, seemed to whirl by her, as did Isabel, who stood against the bookcase with crossed arms. The dance ceased to exist, the music was lost beneath her throbbing senses. Her hostess's fiery mane glazed and shuddered as Augusta moved. Her hands seemed to melt into Sarah. Once, Augusta's bosom brushed incidentally against hers in the course of a half-turn, and a nervous ripple raced up Sarah's back and exploded silvery-blue in the back of her head. She tightened her grip; Lady Pym responded in kind and her lips curved into a smile Sarah knew the others could not feel. She, too, was smiling.

The song ended all to quickly. Augusta released her, slowly and yet too suddenly, nearly panting with the physical exertion. Sarah also found herself short of breath, pleasurably so, though her own condition persisted somewhat longer than the duration of the dance had warranted. Augusta's attention did not leave her.

"Your faith in Sarah seems justified," Isabel sniffed, but this time neither her voice nor the familiar use of her name managed to jar Sarah in the slightest. On the contrary, she scarcely took the time to notice, much less speculate on what if any cutting impression Mrs. Gerard had intended to convey.

Sarah made use of the hour following the guests' departure to write a second letter to Mrs. Waterbury in Bath, again begging her pardon for detouring from her expected course and putting her, perhaps, to some unnecessary worry and bother, but again asking her not to expect her arrival until some further communication. She added a few complimentary descriptions of Lady Pym and her household, which were not at all insincere, and offered blandishments to Mrs. Waterbury's various dependents and children, whom she promised to see soon. She used Lady Pym's specially scented wax to seal the envelope. She felt a particular thrill as she did so, feeling that this simple act had brought her yet closer to her admired hostess. She addressed the letter then, using bold, sweeping strokes of the pen which she seldom allowed her fancy to indulge in. "Too unrestrained," her Uncle Lionel had admonished once, leaning over her desk with a furrowed brow, "not to mention illegible."

She was wondering about Uncle Lionel — surely he had heard of her desertion of Mrs. Waterbury's hospitality by now, or would hear within another day or two — and did not have to stretch her imagination too far to predict his displeasure and mistrust of this unseemly display of independence. Would he write to Augusta? If so, she had little fear that Lady Pym would be in the least withered by his criticisms or implications.

She paused. Implications . . .

The door to the study opened, and Augusta herself strode over to the desk, pausing just behind Sarah's chair. Sarah propped her sealed letter against the inkpot and smiled up at the welcome intruder. She saw that Lady Pym was carrying three leather-bound, oversized books from which protruded a good many scraps of paper and yellowed markers. On some of the exposed bits Sarah could discern numbers.

"Days ago, I promised you a grand tour of my most guarded secrets, dear Sarah. Well —" She plopped the ledgers down on the desk directly in front of Sarah, "— prepare to be dismayed at the appalling state of my affairs. Before you lies every financial blunder with which I have burdened Pym House for the past three years."

"As I said, I am certain I can be of little help. Your solicitors and financial advisors could surely —"

Lady Pym waved a dismissive hand. "What can they possibly say that I couldn't divine for myself? Furthermore, what reason have I to trust them? A widow is a convenient target for all manner of swindle. How Sir Lewis would have burned about the collar to hear of some of the tawdry deals I've nearly been cajoled into accepting."

"Your steward, then, has proven no more reliable?"

"I dismissed my steward three months ago, and have never found another. Isabel has sent hers over from time to time, but he can do only so much. For the most part, I try to manage on my own. Yet I had not the advantage of a banker uncle from whom I might learn by observation. And little, I suspect, slides by your eyes uncaptured, Sarah."

Sarah blinked as Lady Pym moved as if to touch her forehead to illustrate her point. She apparently thought better of it and desisted.

"No steward?" Sarah asked, staring. "That must have been difficult."

"Please. I should greatly value your advice."

"Well, then . . ." Self-consciously, Sarah flipped through the first ledger. Disappointing Lady Pym seemed inevitable. After all, what knowledge had she of finance, which was properly the sphere of gentlemen, or at least of those versed in mathematics? Her governess had, of course, provided the basic instructions for handling household expenses, but errors were as a rule overlooked or only gently chided; since she would presumably marry above herself, a few miscalculations need not dent her husband's store.

She sighed, seeing no escape but to affect an air of competence and blunder through as best she could. Perhaps she could even offer a few harmless suggestions which Lady Pym could smile politely over and later dismiss from her mind.

"Here's something to make notes on." Lady Pym slid some sheets of foolscap and a freshly sharpened quill toward her.

"Oh, thank you. I must remind you that I cannot promise much."

"I shan't require any promises until we've tried."

"Very sensible, I'm sure." Aware that Lady Pym was watching her rather closely, Sarah bent down to an intense study. She read in silence, desperate for the jumbles of figures scattered across an expanse of columns to shift into sense. Then, gradually, an astonishing degree of illumination began to steal over her. Even the numbers on the loose papers wedged between pages seemed to arrange themselves into a particular pattern. During the second hour of her immersion, she ventured a few opinions concerning livestock and gardening expenses, and even voiced an idea about shifting groups of cottagers to better match their personal abilities with the areas of the estate they were to tend.

"For example, the Dove's Nest." She pointed to a series of meager entries in the last column on the page. "You've collected almost no revenue from it for three years."

"That is a problem," Augusta admitted, "but you see, the family there is not well off. The husband is nearly blind, and the wife has three children to tend to. The oldest girl is coming up here next winter, when she's of suitable age, and that will help matters somewhat. I can't ask for more rent, though, unless I were prepared to turn them out. And," she added needlessly, "I am not."

Sarah had a sudden urge to cut her own tongue out. "Of course not," she stammered. "I had no idea."

"Still, let me give it some thought. Perhaps if we asked them to move to the vegetable garden . . ."

A tea tray arrived then, thankfully diverting attention away from Sarah's blunder. They ate and drank in near silence, then turned to the investments page.

"There's five hundred pounds here I can't account for." Sarah scowled, toting the numbers up for the second time. Augusta fidgeted, shifting the empty cups on the tray.

"Well, these discrepancies are bound to happen."

"But five hundred pounds? Did your solicitors notice it, too? Lady Pym, if you have been cheated in the past —"

She shook her head. "No, not in this case. Not in the way you think, anyhow. You're right, perhaps I should have written it down. Why should I hide my transactions, when the money is mine anyway? Here, give me the pen."

Sarah watched as she scratched "C. Ducharme" between two other entries and then "five hundred" in the deficit column beside it.

"The mysterious Miss Ducharme again?"

"The five hundred pounds was my parting gift to her . . . I bought her off, you might say. I'm not proud of it, partially why I couldn't bring myself to record it, but I knew it would be cheaper in the long run. The woman was bleeding me dry, you see. Gowns and loans to her friends, betting on horses against Roderick Finch . . . oh, it was endless."

"But who was she? Why were you obligated to cover her debts for her? Even if she were kin . . ."

"She wasn't. I met her at a house party in Wales, just before last Christmas. I brought her back here to spend the winter. Unfortunately, she spent much more than that."

"And you never tried to stop her?" Sarah was amazed, but at the same time realized it was hardly her place to criticize Lady Pym's spending. Five hundred pounds was probably nothing to her. "Forgive me, I know it's none of my concern."

"My only excuse is that I'm as likely as the next person to be led astray by the heart. I loved Miss Ducharme, you see. I only regret it now because she so clearly had no regard for me."

"Oh." Humiliation was too mild a word for what now engulfed Sarah. Swallowing hard, she picked up her pen again. "Well, the numbers do add up now."

Laughing, Lady Pym plucked the pen out of her hand and tossed it to the furthest corner of the desk. "Poor Sarah, you're so earnest. We've done enough for today, though it's been very profitable. Let's take it up again tomorrow."

Sarah remained perfectly still, her fingers remaining curved as if holding the pen shaft. She stared at Augusta.

"You always look so . . . wounded." Augusta brushed a stray black lock back behind Sarah's ear.

"Did . . . Miss Ducharme also help you with your books?"

"Never. I may have been a fool where she was concerned, but I've never been outright stupid."

"I'm sure you haven't." Sarah couldn't help smiling. An odd fancy seized her then, leading her to believe that Lady Pym's flame-colored tresses, hanging loose over her shoulders, might actually be warm to the touch. Irrational though this was, Sarah could not resist trying. Holding her breath, she slid both hands into that cascading mane. Lady Pym tilted her head back amazingly, in full compliance. Then, when Sarah let go, so on fire herself she couldn't tell what the temperature of the hair had been, Augusta slid forward in turn.

Sarah shivered with pleasure when she felt the first moist pressure on her mouth. The sweetness was overpowering. It reminded her of a childhood afternoon, when she had plucked a purple wildflower and put it curiously into her mouth. Its juices had made her lips tingle and burn all at once. At that point her governess, who had been daydreaming on her own, realized what she had done and had shaken her roughly, ordering her to expel it. Not on the path, she had shrilled, for that would have been hardly ladylike. "In your handkerchief, Miss, right this instant!"

Lady Pym broke away and sat up again. There was no bitter aftertaste this time. Sarah's senses seemed awash with nectar. She was floating, floating, like one of Mr. Tennyson's indolent Lotus-Eaters. "Augusta," she whispered.

The import of what had happened struck her only several seconds later. The blow was like that of a hammer. She gaped at Augusta, who sat before her composed, making no effort at further contact.

Sarah struggled for breath, as well as for understanding.

"This must seem very strange to you," Augusta said gently.

"Oh, my dear Lord," blustered Sarah. She wriggled out of the desk chair. Augusta rose much less awkwardly and stood between Sarah and the only possible route to the door.

"Your fear is to be expected," she went on, still in that level, reasoning tone of voice. This fact only disoriented Sarah more. How many times had Lady Pym found herself in such a . . . situation, after all? "But be assured, Sarah, it is not some horrible, life-sucking fervor leading straight to hell, or the grave. I have spent half my life learning that."

"I have . . . heard of such women." As you, she had started to say. As me. Tears rained down her face, through her being. "But they were indecent, not fit to be respectable people —"

"No one in my house, Sarah, shall ever ask you to do, much less feel, anything which your will opposes. You are my guest. I did not bring this about by design, I swear to you."

"Perhaps it is as much my fault." An image of that leering mother-spectre who had accosted her in the night returned to Sarah. This was her doing, too. Uncle Lionel had not, after all, misjudged the infernos that waited, smoldering, in her lineage.

Lady Pym's complacency vanished suddenly. Gripping Sarah with one hand, with the other she scooped up the letter which still rested innocuously on the inkpot. "Here," she said, a blush spreading across her forehead in frustration, "your letter. I shall tear it for you, tear it and scatter the pieces. Go to Bath tomorrow, if you want. I'll make all the arrangements." She made a move as if to shred it.

"No, please!" Sarah lurched for it, and Augusta allowed her to snatch it away. Sarah pressed it against her middle and leaned against the desk, breathing hard. All her limbs were shaking, but she forced them to stop. "I . . . have no wish to leave for Bath tomorrow," she whispered. "But I must be alone for a time, Lady Pym, do you understand that?"

"Yes." Sarah moved to the doorway.

Lady Pym did not oppose her at first, then she touched her arm. "Don't go to your room, I beg you. It is no place to consider such a matter. You must not close yourself in. That is how you have spent your whole life, do you see? Go anywhere else. The gardens, perhaps, the orchards. Be out in God's Nature, with nothing between you and Him."

"It has always been my belief that God can see us through any walls," Sarah murmured with a vague smile.

Lady Pym arched her thin eyebrows. "Well, then, some startling sights He's surely had."

They both laughed a little, and Augusta left her.

As she heard Lady Pym retreat, Sarah found herself alone. She decided to put as much distance between herself and the scene of her current indiscretion as she could. She had to admit that Lady Pym's suggestion of avoiding her room was a sound one: she had never approved of pining in solitude. At home, if she found herself in a pet, she was far more likely to head to the stables, where the groom would steady her hand and allow her to feed bits of sweet to Sandy, her small mare. Or she might wander to the edge of their property and watch the children romping in the adjoining garden. Uncle Lionel never offered hospitality to those people, because he could not abide the noise children made. Yet she sometimes found their screams of abandon, and their total acceptance of whatever fantasy they chose to create on that day, reassuring. Once, one of the girls had even declared herself Good Queen Bess, and demanded the others flatter her accordingly. Her darker, tousle-headed sister had remained stubbornly seated on the ground, and asserted, "I am a blood-thirsting Spaniard spy, then." "Miss Redding!" Queen Bess had swung back to their patient, observing nurse in annoyance. "She can't really be a spy, can she?"

Of course, Sarah thought, none of the matters weighing on her mind then could possibly have been half as grave, as shameful, as this.

The sunlight, dimming as early evening approached, warmed her flushed cheeks as she stepped out into the garden. As she walked, she did begin to feel better. She listened to the echoes of birdsong, and the rhythmic buzz of insects, humming all around her. A spotted cat, crouching in some rosebushes by the gate, jumped up and darted away as she approached. She found it difficult to imagine any note of chastisement or stricture in any of these aspects of their God's greater World.

As she stepped through the gate, she realized that Lady Pym must be in the habit, too, of visiting her stables during occasions of distress. She apparently did not stop at offering her animals treats, however. For, even as Sarah watched, Lady Pym thundered across the landscape in her bottle-green riding cloak and hat, seated on the largest chalk-white mount Sarah had ever observed.

CHAPTER 7

Isabel Gerard was seated before her mirror, an array of toiletries spread out before her, humming to herself in an abstracted mood while a servant patiently brushed and re-curled her hair. The wind, whipping against Angela's open carriage as they'd rumbled home at a most exhilarating speed, had tangled it almost beyond recognition, and she had, of course, no intention of joining the supper table in such a disheveled state. She stopped humming and caught her breath in discomfort as the girl accidentally pulled on the roots. Isabel reached back and slapped the kneading fingers lightly. "Silly thing, you know I'm not fond of pain."

"My apologies, madam —"

"Oh, well, never mind." Isabel now patted the hand she had chastised. "You do your best, well I know, but I'm simply impossible. I do try not to be unreasonable. But tell me truly, dear, will the blue gown do for dinner?"

"Oh, yes, madam, with the new lace it will suit you most handsomely. Mr. Gerard will be stunned."

Isabel shrilled a laugh. "That would be most satisfactory, though I cannot expect it." Privately she conjured a rather grotesque image of Sylvan gaping lustfully at her across a laden dinner table, his tiny spectacles slipping lower on his nose, his thin lower lip hanging ruddy and inarticulate. "Good heavens," she chortled aloud, wrapping up the entertaining fantasy with a mental bow and colored paper and stowing it away for later use. Another maid knocked and entered the room with a curtsy.

"Lady Pym, madam," the girl announced.

"What? Oh, for heaven's sakes." Isabel glanced at the mirror, then pulled a strand of hair tentatively onto her forehead. "Give it a twist, dear, just something that will tumble lightly over my eyebrow. Mind you, I don't want it straggling."

"Yes'm." The girl dipped at the knees, biting her lower lip.

A few minutes later, parts of her scalp still stinging from the aftereffects of haste, Isabel came onto her landing to see Augusta, still in her cloak, pacing back and forth near the bottom step. Isabel descended at a more leisured pace. Augusta's head jerked up, and Isabel saw the agitation in her posture and in her taut, sudden movements.

"High time you came down here!"

"Why didn't those silly chits show you to the drawing room? God's blood, the servants I get these days." She shook her gold head in an affected manner. "Thought I'd be deprived of my scalp just now, too."

"I didn't want to sit," Augusta sputtered, wheeling around and charging into the next room.

Isabel followed. "Oh ho. Trouble at the palace, my liege?"

Augusta was picking up ornaments at random, turning them over once in her hands, and plunking them down again as though she had entered some substandard auction. "I must talk, Iz, I simply must."

"What would you like to drink?" Isabel reached for the bell-rope.

"Anything." Augusta flung out her arm, turning on her heel again. "Whatever you're having, I mean."

Isabel pursed her lips. "Claret, I think. Not the best hour for it, perhaps, but at least I'll be able to laugh over Sylvan's silly jokes at dinner."

"Fine, fine, claret then." Augusta threw herself onto a low French sofa, then proceeded to stare at her feet with an odd intensity as Isabel gave *sotto voce* instructions to the maid. Isabel waited until they were alone again, then came and sat down, very close, to her sulky guest.

104

"So," she stated baldly, "you love Miss Lindsay, then?"

"Good God!" Augusta sputtered. A flush that matched her hair spread over her cheeks.

"Do you take me for ignorant all of a sudden? I know your emotions as well as you know them yourself, probably better in some cases. And you have always known what you felt, Augusta."

Augusta stared at her, gradually regaining her composure. "No, Iz, you mistake me. I've never doubted your perceptiveness. For once, though, I simply don't know where to begin."

"With Miss Lindsay, of course. Does she understand what you wish of her? If not, perhaps you had better tell her before some dreadful misunderstanding occurs."

Augusta's cloudy eyes flashed anew. "Sarah is hardly ignorant, either."

"In other words, she responds."

"She . . . well, yes, she has. She kissed my hand, in any case. But I don't know whence those responses arise."

"And what did you do? You wanted her to kiss you, I presume."

Augusta's cross expression was almost instantly replaced by a wistful smile. "Most certainly I did. She is perfectly lovely, Iz, in every way I could wish. I know that she would never make a fool of me in the way that Miss Ducharme was only too happy to do. She has a wonderful heart, Iz, and a great soul. She fears injuring me almost as much as I fear . . . doing her harm."

"By loving her, do you mean? What nonsense,

Augusta. How can love do anyone any harm? Even Miss Lindsay, with her marvelous soul, must see that."

"She is still quite innocent, Iz."

"We are all born with an astounding capacity to learn. And I, for one, am well familiar with your endless patience, Lady Pym."

Augusta fell silent, different concerns nudging into her mind. She stood, crossed the room a few times, then leaned against the tall maple hutch in the corner which Isabel used to display a silver platter.

"Am I causing you pain, then, by speaking of this? I've always been aware that I disclose my feelings somewhat hastily, without considering my words' effect on others. Still, as you always tell me, we cannot circumvent our natures. Do accept my apologies, dear, if I've hurt you. I suppose I've never grown unaccustomed to thinking of you as a tangible part of me, rather like an additional limb really."

"No, no." Isabel shook herself fiercely, then lapsed into a discreet silence as a chubby maid entered with a decanter and glasses on an engraved tray. When she was gone, Isabel studied her fingernails. "When I set you free, darling, I knew you'd love others. God's blood, why wouldn't you? Especially with dear Lewis's steady stream of associates bubbling through your hallowed halls . . ."

"And you had Sylvan, of course. I accepted that, too."

"We were each very fair with each other. I believe that, don't you?"

Augusta wandered around the room, then returned to her seat and sipped from her glass. "We both knew Sylvan would never understand."

"He would never be like Sir Lewis, with his benign little Ganymedes, no. That's why I wouldn't let you make me a match. I couldn't have borne that. I wanted Sylvan to adore me — yes, I admit that, and why should I be ashamed? To imagine, even for a moment, that those glassy looks he gives me were really for the likes of that dreadful Leslie person, or that shaggy-headed artist . . ."

"Never mind that," Augusta cut her off abruptly. "Lewis and I were well-suited, weren't we? I'd not be here with you now were we not. And whatever his faults may have been — well, they're dust along with him now."

Isabel nursed her own glass for a while. "Do you often miss what we had? Or did you, very much, in the beginning?"

"I knew nothing of love before you. Dalliance, maybe."

The response was guarded. Isabel knew that tone. "I was a fine rehearsal for Miss Lindsay, then. To her health."

Augusta did not return the salute. Instead, she sighed and tapped the side of her foot against the carpet. "I'm afraid that she would die of shame, Iz. The upbringing she's had — that uncle, from all I've heard . . ."

"Oh?" Isabel's golden eyebrows arched. "And were we brought up much differently, then?"

"Well, we had each other." A tiny laugh, more like the usual Augusta, escaped her drawn lips.

"And Miss Lindsay has you. She's very lucky I relinquished you, in a way."

"You are too dreadful." Bursting into a smile all at once, Augusta leaned over and kissed Isabel's warm, smooth forehead. "Sylvan isn't."

The sound of masculine knuckles, heavily ringed, thudded from the threshold. Before either could answer, the door creaked open and Roderick Finch appeared, leaning back against it, his face somewhat blotchy and his plaid cravat askew. His puffy pink eyes regarded their decanter with overt interest.

"Heard you were here, Lady Pym, thought I'd pay my respects. In one's own house, and all . . ."

"You're not making any sense, Rod," Isabel snapped, "and you're mumbling."

"Oh, piffle." Striding into the room, Roderick flopped down in a chair, remembering to spread his coattails over his legs only at the last moment. He sighed plaintively. "Always railing at me, isn't she." Again he eyed the claret. "Give us one of those, won't you, Isabel? There's a dear."

Saying something under her breath, Isabel complied. When she handed him the glass, some of it splashed onto his trousers. "God's blood," he wailed, in a perfect imitation of his sister.

"Perhaps you'd better go and clean off."

"Oh, that's your game. Well, I'll be off soon enough, never worry. But I mustn't slight Lady Pym."

"You'd have offended her less had you simply kept to the smoking room."

Roderick ignored her, offering only a snort in reply. Instead he turned fully toward Augusta. "You have a charming guest still with you, I understand.

She came to tea just recently. So very well-mannered. Good family, Izzy says."

"She's correct."

"Well, one can always tell. I was most impressed, I tell you, most impressed."

Isabel observed tartly, "Anyone would seem well-bred to Rod. Anyone who didn't jump into his lap and bare at least her ankle to him."

"A very fetching pair of ears," Rod blithered. He had begun blinking, as though keeping his swollen lids open was becoming more difficult as each moment fled. "Like little white shells, the sort one finds in Italy."

"As if you could appreciate shells, or any vessel not deep enough to hold a draught of ale. But enough of all this, Rod. Miss Lindsay is off limits to you. I understand she's promised to someone already."

"Oh, and what matter that?" In an incredible display of indelicacy, Rod fished through his waistcoat pockets for his snuff-box, which he proceeded to make use of without any apologies whatsoever. "Certainly she can't love the fellow. There's no more love in England, haven't you heard?"

"Good Lord, get out of here." Isabel stood up, reaching toward the bell-pull, as Rod began to hunt for his handkerchief. "I'll have you removed to bed if you don't go yourself, Rod, I swear it. Would you really like to be carried?"

Rod found his handkerchief, blew his nose, and heaved himself resignedly to his feet. "Well, my commendations to Miss Lindsay, then. Will you stay to dine, Lady Pym?"

"No, I think not."

"Ah, another time perhaps. Did I mention you're looking quite ruddy yourself these days? Though I must put in a word for the consumptive complexion, which is all the rage in London. Such a face would complement mine better, don't you think? But enough, Isabel! I'm off!" He went.

Isabel slammed the door after him. "Imagine the nerve! If he comes to call on you, Augusta, I shan't be at all put out if you do precisely that to him."

"I'll remember it. But as I said, I don't believe Sarah is ignorant."

"Go back to her, then. Sylvan will be here within the hour, and I must finish dressing."

"Very well." Augusta walked back into the foyer, and waited as the servants returned her hat and riding gloves. She rebuttoned her cloak, which she had kept on in all the distraction, and trotted down the steps with her composure restored.

Isabel moved back into the drawing room to watch her guest's mount barrel off down the hill again. In the distance, she could just discern Sylvan's small carriage jolting along at a more sedate pace.

"Anna!" she called, heading quickly back to her dressing room. "My gown, please. Mr. Gerard will be home soon . . ."

Sarah was enduring a joyless cup of tea, seated alone at the little stone table in the corner of the garden, when the first raindrops touched her neck and shoulders. She shivered, pushing her teacup away, but did not rise until Valerie came dashing out to take the tray.

"Oh, but you'd better get inside, Miss. You'll be soaked to the skin!"

"Yes." Her lips formed words slowly; they sounded distant even to her own ears. "You're quite right."

Valerie paused, tray in hands, a silvery drop trickling down the side of her face and onto her collar. Sarah watched that sliding drop, and the pale skin beneath it. Involuntarily, she flinched.

"There, you're shivering already," Valerie pronounced with satisfaction. "And you are looking so very sad, Miss."

"I do feel a little tired."

"It's all this company, I'm sure. One of the kitchen girls was telling me how it was when old Sir Lewis was alive. No rest for any of them, she was saying. All manner of people running in and out. You'd never fancy him so popular, to judge from his picture, would you? They'd cluster in that book-room for hours on end, talking and talking, singing even. Not quite right, somehow, if you ask me. People ought to be more sedate, and all."

"Like Uncle Lionel, you mean."

"Well, Miss, it's not really my place to say."

"Perhaps it was Lady Pym they came to see."

Not wishing to hear Valerie's reply, Sarah heaved herself to her feet at last and preceded her damp maid into the house.

She wandered into the salon. The light had faded more than she'd realized, sitting outdoors, for the hulking shapes of the furniture loomed silent before her in a vaguely threatening attitude. She ran a

111

tentative hand across the piano. Its polished coolness tingled up her arm. On this very spot, almost, she had first found herself drawn into her hostess's intoxicating embrace . . .

"Valerie . . ."

Valerie had not yet vanished with the tray. "Yes, Miss? Something else?"

"Yes. Send Madame Lothaire to me, here. Tell her I wish a book from the locked case, and to bring the keys. Certainly she has some."

"I'll tell her, Miss." She peered at her mistress in obvious confusion. "Shall I light you a candle, then? It's dark in here, isn't it."

"Not just yet, Valerie, thank you. I'll wait for Madame Lothaire."

"As you wish, Miss." Shaking her head, Valerie bore the tray off to the kitchen.

Alone again, and welcoming the silence, Sarah sank onto the sofa and half-closed her eyes. Isabel Gerard had occupied this very spot, not so very long ago. Sarah saw again the picture she had conjured then: Augusta and Isabel, side by side, laughing together. Augusta might reach up to swipe playfully at a golden curl. Sarah could not shake the burning in the pit of her abdomen as the image drifted in and out of her mind, along with half-recalled strains of Angela Lamb's concerto, and the pressure of Augusta's arms around her own waist.

The piano beckoned from the shadows, and she slid onto the bench, resting her fingers on the keyboard. She remembered enough of Angela's piece to manage a brief, tolerable imitation of it, though the words remained beyond her abilities both linguistic and musical. If she could set them to

English, she mused, what would they be? Something soft, and romantic, not inappropriately carnal but expressing the depths of devotion between a woman and her beloved.

Sarah paused, folding her hands under her chin in annoyance. What, after all, knew she of forming such words? No passion had ever inspired her, no lover had spoken such flatteries to her, unless she counted Mr. Hyde's banal fawnings at the birthday party and before then. She would never endure him again, that much she had already decided. Whatever Uncle Lionel's objections, she would put the entire suit to rest as soon as she returned home. No uncertainties with respect to her future reputation or behavior would ever induce her to settle for so horrible an incarceration. At least Lady Pym's regard had convinced her that she might deserve the same from others, as well. If any of her suitors had ever produced in her the same churningly warm, all-consuming emotions as did Lady Pym!

Embarrassment, and the heaviness of that afternoon crept, insidious, through every inch of her. Her lips and tongue, especially, blazed with the memorized imprint of that afternoon's indiscretion. Sarah touched the very place with her hand, half expecting to ignite.

The salon door squeaked open abruptly; Sarah nearly leapt from the piano bench.

"Miss Lindsay wished some assistance?" Madame Lothaire inquired in her patient manner, standing in the threshold. Sarah was grateful for the darkness obscuring each of them. Swallowing, she tried to will her blush away.

"Yes, that's right," she managed after a moment.

"I'd better light some candles. Will it please Miss to wait here a short time?"

"Yes, yes, that will be fine."

"Thank you, Miss." Madame Lothaire bent respectfully at the waist and moved into the foyer for a candle. Sarah got up from the piano and moved to the window. The grounds were entirely black now, and the rain spurted down the windowpanes with steadily increasing fury.

"Has Lady Pym not returned from her riding yet?" she inquired as Madame Lothaire bent over the candelabrum on the center table.

"No, Miss, not so far as I'm aware."

"But the storm — surely she shouldn't be out in it, and in the dark, too —"

"If the weather proves too threatening for her, which is not often the case, Lady Pym will no doubt seek temporary shelter with Mrs. Gerard. We have learned not to worry in such cases. If Miss is concerned about dinner . . ."

"No, no, I'm not at all hungry. I was concerned about Lady Pym's safety. But I'm sure you're quite correct not to be disturbed."

"I didn't say that, exactly." Lothaire straightened, and flashed her pearly little teeth at Sarah in a semblance of a friendly smile. "Now, what did Miss wish from the cabinet?"

"Well, it was this one." Sarah pointed to the rows of supposedly scientific treatises. "A certain title caught my eye this morning, and I wish to examine it now that I am at my leisure."

"Madam guards those volumes very carefully." Lothaire's words carried the unmistakable air of a warning. Sarah was determined to ignore it, if only to convince Lothaire of her own innocence in the matter.

"Lady Pym is aware that I wished to look at them." She risked injecting a certain harshness into her next statement. "Are you afraid I might do them some harm, Madame Lothaire?"

"Certainly not, Miss." Lothaire's cheeks flushed a little this time. Taking an impressive bundle of keys into her hand, she unlocked the cabinet, opened the glass doors, and stepped away. "I shall leave Miss to browse as she wishes. Please summon me personally if there is anything further. No doubt Lady Pym has informed Miss of the age of some of these volumes, and the necessity of handling each with the utmost care."

"Quite so. Thank you, Madame, I'm sure you have many other things to attend to." Sarah deliberately turned her back on the housekeeper, and scanned the books with affected nonchalance. Lothaire took the hint and closed the door discreetly as she left.

Sarah's heart began to pound with guilt and excitement, much as it had in Sir Lewis's room. She slid out one slim, vellum-bound volume and flipped it open at random. She did the same with a second, and a third. By the time she had hold of the fourth, her hands were shaking. Where had a woman of Lady Pym's refinement ever got possession of such works? Through their pages roamed women, and some men, whose behavior could be termed uninhibited only by the most charitable reader. Here were women who strode about in trousers, smoked pipes before company, and loved one another quite openly — not with the innocuous fervor of Lucy

Gwinn and her Dorothy, but with a depth of passion, and in some cases a candidness of affection, that surpassed even the most ardent declarations between men and women in more conventional novels.

Some of the books were in French, and had illustrations, and most seemed to have been privately published. Those in Latin she did not even open for fear of what she might see. At one point, she actually ceased to breathe, upon noticing what appeared to be her own name in print, attributed to just such a protagonist. It was a long moment before she bent closer and discerned that the name was actually *Anna*.

While she perused, the rain continued to gush against the house, and the floor under her seemed to shudder as the night groaned with thunder. The mantle-clock's ornate hands spun around once, and then again, and by then Sarah found herself planted in the corner chair, one of the books on her knees, reading feverishly. This particular story concerned two women raised in fine homes situated side by side — reluctantly she thought of Augusta and Isabel — who grew gradually into a closeness which, they assured one another, would one day surpass death. When one of the women returned from a short journey to find her friend betrothed, she poured out a torrent of words in which Sarah heard, for perhaps the first time in any work of fiction she had read, the truth of her own soul, framed to perfection in words. She felt complete empathy as she clung to this passage. She heard a gurgle of emotion in her throat.

Again the room shivered against an enormous peal of thunder. One of the French doors blew open, rebounding against the wall. Sarah dropped the book on the floor and leaped to her feet as a looming figure crashed in from the downpour. The candles illuminated the swirl of a bottle-green cloak just as Sarah was about to scream. Lady Pym stood hunched before her, dripping.

"I saw you as I was crossing the lawn." Her hostess shrugged as she removed her hat and sent a shower of water over the carpet. "I decided not to present myself at the front door and endure Madame Lothaire's wrath. She cannot abide a wet foyer."

Sarah saw Augusta's gaze travel the length of her body, and settle on the small volume which lay splayed and upside down beside her. The doors of the bookcase stood open behind her. Sarah scooped up the dropped book. "I made Madame Lothaire open it," she stammered in shame. "I wanted something to read, you see, and I —"

"May I see it?" Augusta reached for the book. When Sarah surrendered it, thoroughly abashed, Augusta flipped it over, turned a few pages, and smiled. "Yes, a particular favorite of mine. I once met the woman who wrote it, you know. She's getting old now, of course, and her authorship is not a well-known fact. Still, I was determined to find her. I finally came upon her in Scotland — sitting alone, and watching the sea-birds. I could not have conjured a more perfect scenario."

She glanced up at Sarah who stared back, rapt. "She . . . was surprised that I knew who she was, but I assured her my search hadn't been easy. She asked me why I'd persisted. I told her that I'd waited all my life to encounter someone, particularly a woman, who knew how to write truly of love."

After some time, Sarah nodded. "She does know," she agreed. "I felt that, too."

Augusta smiled, and read out the very speech Sarah had absorbed so desperately. " 'I have known nothing of love until these hours with you. When we are apart it seems as though my heart is warning me that it shall cease to beat, as though my limbs are dissolving, and I am rendered purest soul; a soul which seeks to drift, and drift, past this life and this cage of our aloneness, and repose instead with yours, curling together like infants, yet with the knowledge of all life within us.' " Augusta smiled again, closed the book, and set it on the piano. "Well, I don't claim to be a Dr. Johnson. Still, that seems to me something he would never understand, and the work is all the richer for it."

"No doubt you are right." Sarah felt a sweat bead just above her upper lip. Lady Pym's private amusement drained away, and was replaced by a different look, which Sarah had seen before.

"I . . . I myself might have spoken such words to you this morning, had I possessed perfect recall, Sarah."

"That is a skill I do not prize. One's own words are always preferable." Gazing at her, Sarah added, "I would have rather heard those."

The two drifted closer. "And would you hear them now?"

"Only if you will hear mine, Augusta," Sarah murmured. "As I warned you long ago, however, I shall never be a poet."

"I have a dozen poets at arm's length, when I am in this room. It is not a poet I require, at this particular moment."

Sarah released her soul into her words: "You may have whatever you want." Slowly, as though she were acting in a dream, Sarah opened her arms. Augusta moved into them, and her wet cape enveloped them both.

In the near-darkness of the tower room, Augusta peeled away her damp garments while Sarah watched, perched rigid at the edge of the bed. The crooks of her elbows and knees were slick with fear. Her fingers mangled the spread. She couldn't help staring as Augusta moved closer, for she had never seen a fully unclothed person, even another woman, before her. The sight was more soul-striking than any discreetly draped marble could ever prove.

Augusta seemed not to mind her brazen eyes. Her white skin shone phantomlike as she settled beside Sarah. "Hold me," she said, guiding Sarah's tense arms around her.

"I want to please you." Sarah swallowed. This was the truth; yet how could she hope to satisfy this woman, who had been loved by the brilliant Isabel Gerard and the worldly Miss Ducharme?

"You couldn't help but make me happy." Augusta plucked at the strings of Sarah's tight petticoat. "You are in my heart, everywhere."

Sarah's flesh prickled as the night's coolness, and then Augusta's hands, touched her. Steady palms slipped warmly along the upward curve of her breasts. They paused.

"Sarah," Augusta said seriously, pushing her to arm's length for a moment, "if I hurt you, or frighten you, you must tell me at once. If you decide that you want me to stop, I will."

"No." Sarah swallowed, her shivering body urging her mind to relinquish those last shreds of propriety which seemed so hopelessly out of place suddenly. "I want you to love me."

"I do — I will." Augusta's hands began to move again then, trailing over Sarah's front with a bold pressure that made her gasp. She in turn pressed closer to Augusta's warmth, biting back a surge of nervous panic. She trailed her fingers along either side of Augusta's spine, and felt the quick tightening of muscle there.

Augusta, too, shuddered with pleasure, then looped the bedclothes around them both and rolled onto the pillows. She pulled Sarah along, the last bits of restrictive clothing tumbling from between them. Sarah felt an insistent tongue slip along her tender throat, and instinctively locked her knees around Augusta's. She felt the curve of a smile transform Augusta's kiss against her shoulder.

"As when we danced," she whispered into yielding flesh. "I have much to teach you, Miss Lindsay."

"There is much I wish to learn."

"You shall." Augusta stretched her body evenly alongside Sarah's, then ran a touch as light as feathers down the curve of her side and back up the inside of her thigh. Sarah had to bite back an undignified squeal of happiness. The heel of Augusta's hand began to roughly massage the slight protrusion of her hipbone, sending a series of chills through her. She realized that Augusta, too, was murmuring in a smartingly abandoned manner, then felt her tongue once again, this time against her breasts. Her back gave an involuntary lurch as intrepid fingers moved steadily down the faint trail of dark hair on her lower abdomen, then curled between her thighs. Sarah could not help but writhe in enjoyment as Lady Pym's persistent probings roused her to an ecstacy she had never imagined possible. Why, why had such divine acts ever been condemned by those misguided creatures who dictated the rules of human society? The last thing she would ever feel with regard to Augusta, she vowed, was the guilt others would surely try to impose upon her if they knew.

As her excitement grew, Sarah began to take her cue from Lady Pym and to return her ardent caresses. Soon nothing existed for her save Augusta's damp, convulsing body, and she could see by Augusta's half-closed but glassy eyes that the same was true for her. Slowly, a fiery hand began to close around her insides and spread its wild flame all the way up to her throat. This time she was unable to stifle the cry that wrenched itself from her, and she felt her fingernails drag against Augusta's rigid sides. Augusta, too, was lost in a prolonged moan.

Presently both collapsed back into the pillows, breathing hard, every nerve almost audibly singing. Lady Pym's protective arms slid back around Sarah.

She felt tears sting her face. "I — I never knew . . ." she began to whisper, but was too exhausted to complete the sentence, or to try and explain the myriad of wondrous feelings that churned within her, everywhere.

"Sleep now," Augusta coaxed, her own voice weak but a bit more coherent. She continued to stroke Sarah's loose long hair, kissing her eyelids closed, and Sarah reveled in the sensation until the warmth of sleep crept over her and all was silent.

CHAPTER 8

The outline of the tower room drifted in a damp gray haze that held a faintly metallic taste. One of the sheets, freed from its moorings during the night, was wound around Sarah's left calf, while a tangle of blankets had successfully captured her torso. In addition, her right arm lay wedged beneath Augusta Pym's ribcage. The sharp prickle under her skin, and the near-numbness of her fingers, suggested that it had best be extracted forthwith. Trying not to wake Augusta, and thus jar that steady breathing and heartbeat, Sarah placed her free hand on the sleeper's shoulder, and tried to tug her arm gradually loose. Augusta stirred, sighed, and woke after all.

"I'm sorry," Sarah whispered, then displayed her swollen arm. "This is all I needed."

Augusta ran her hand along Sarah's wrist. "One of the disadvantages to these situations. Someone always runs the risk of losing a limb."

Sarah smiled, but averted her eyes. Augusta, sliding closer, embraced her in silence, and Sarah pressed against her willingly, tipping her face into the shower of red hair which dropped over them both like a veil. Warmth cocooned them, despite the chill of the morning.

"I feel as though I'm holding a flame," Sarah said finally, taking a handful of scented locks.

"The flames of Purgatorio?" Augusta laughed, lifting herself a little. Sarah shook her head, again shifting her gaze. Augusta kissed her on the throat, and fell back again with a resigned sigh.

"Being in this room is a bit like being trapped in a bottle, isn't it?" she asked, staring up. Sarah studied the ceiling, too, and the series of tapestries, including the one with the singed corner, which ranged around them. She forced the thought of Isabel from her mind.

"I ought to get up," Augusta was saying. "It will be easier if I go back to my own room for a while." She tossed the bedclothes back and rolled to her feet. She walked to the window, Sarah covertly admiring her firm white back, and the boldness with which she flipped back the curtains and opened the casements. A breath of chilly dawn air whistled between them. "Mornings are always the same out here, whatever time of year," she grumbled. "I think we're done with the rain, though. That's good."

Sarah stifled a laugh. "I think the time for conversations involving the climate is long past."

"No, I've a reason for wondering. You'll see later." Augusta strode to the dresser, where the jug stood partially full. She poured the water into the basin and sloshed some over her face. She never winced at its iciness, though Sarah flinched in sympathy. Sarah then stared in amazement as Augusta picked up the jug again, took a mouthful, and matter-of-factly spit it out of the open window. "After all, it is my house," she challenged, "and nobody's up yet to see me. I'm borrowing your dressing gown, incidentally."

"Yes, all right." Sarah's consent was superfluous; Augusta already had the robe on. Seeing her in it pleased Sarah.

"You'll want your nightdress, too, when your Valerie arrives," Augusta said. "Shall I help you with it?"

"I could scarcely ring for someone else." Sarah stood up and moved to the mirror, wondering if she would face a stranger's reflection. Yet she still appeared much the same, albeit a little disheveled. Augusta stole up behind her and yanked the nightdress down over her head. The crisp linen, and Augusta's touch, made her shiver again. Augusta's arms slid around her waist.

Sarah asked, "Do you think all the servants will know?"

"Madame Lothaire will. She knows everything that happens here. That's all to the good, however. She'll see to it that no one else interferes."

125

"What was it you told her last night, before we went up?" Such practicalities would never have occurred to Sarah, or at least not until the opportunity for discretion was lost. Again she was grateful for Lady Pym's poise, and even her experience, in such matters. Sarah saw Augusta smile. The two women were rocking slowly in front of the mirror now.

"I told her we would be reading together into the night and would see ourselves off. That was enough. She is very perceptive."

Had she used such excuses when she had gone upstairs to meet Isabel Finch? Sarah smothered a frown. Instead she cleared her throat. "Augusta?"

"Yes, love?"

"Is it very different with — with a man?" Sarah blushed, and swallowed. "Forgive me, but I . . . wondered."

"A little different, yes. Not that my experience has been so extensive."

"But surely . . . I mean, you were a wife for many years."

"True, but Sir Lewis and I had what you might call an arrangement in that respect. He was fifteen years older than I, though he seldom would admit it, and when it became apparent that we would not produce an heir, we reverted with complete contentment to what we had always intended, a union based on friendship."

"I see." Sarah did not see, but could bear to inquire no further. She had never heard of a man, especially one of Sir Lewis's status, accepting the lack of a son so complacently. Certainly the need for one had occasioned more matches, and even some separations, than the sort of amity Augusta described. Instead, she reverted to her original line of questioning. "Somehow," she ventured, her throat growing dry with embarrassment, "I expect it would be a good deal less . . . gentle. I could never really come to know . . . a man the way I have you, Augusta."

"Because that's the way men have arranged it. Most of us are forced to bide by their dogmas in some respects, even those as fortunate as I. For some, of course, that is sufficient. If genuine love can blossom under such circumstances, and I'm well assured it does, so be it. But it never could for me."

"I always wondered why I had never fallen in love the way most of my friends did. When we went to parties or dinners, they would stand together in groups and admire the most ridiculous young men, who sat braying for hours over gallons of wine, stiff as tailors' dummies in their fine cravats and coattails. All the time, merely pretending to find them diverting, I would stare at the carpet, or more often the clocks."

A shadow of concern flickered through Augusta's eyes. Sarah noticed it, despite the intervention of the mirror.

"You're young yet to entirely discount love with a man. You might still find it, and be all the happier for it."

Sarah turned, slowly initiating a much fuller embrace. "I discounted it long ago. And I have already found all the love I desire."

"And I. And I." They clung together for several minutes. Then Augusta tipped her head toward the window. "Look, it's less gray now. The first servants will be up any time. I'll be in the breakfast hall when you get up." Gently extricating herself, Augusta kissed Sarah's smooth forehead. "Poor thing, you're so tired."

"No," Sarah protested, even though it was true. Laughing again, Augusta let herself out and padded down the silent hall. Sarah sat back down on the bed, huddling against the cold. Her eyes drooped heavily. Gradually, a misty face formed itself near the window.

"A pleasant morning, dear daughter?" Her mother's wide, dark lips were smirking.

They breakfasted later than usual, for Sarah had, somewhat to her own surprise, slept like death after Augusta's departure from the tower room. The two faced each other across the white tablecloth, saying little, smiling in shared secrecy as various dishes were carted before them. Only the vague recollection of her odd morning dream threatened Sarah's complacency. She felt uncomfortable concealing the matter of her background from Augusta. One day, she was bound to hear from someone why one of Sarah's standing was fit only for suitors of Mr. Ian Hyde's caliber. Yet for now she was paralyzed. Even imagining a horrified reaction on Augusta's face was too painful to endure.

"The good weather has held," Augusta said finally, turning to gaze out the long, white-curtained windows. She drummed her fingers briefly on the table. Sarah resolutely shoved all unpleasantries to the darkest caverns of her mind. "We'll go straight out when we're done here, shall we? The grass may be a bit damp, but we'll never mind that."

"I shan't mind."

They strolled out together, crossing the garden at a brisk pace and heading directly into the orchard. Augusta kept her arm around Sarah's waist, and Sarah leaned against her in complete happiness. Again, they maintained a relative silence, Augusta watching the changing sky and Sarah unable to harness the tide of emotion within her long enough, or fully enough, to complete even one coherent phrase.

She also feared she might demonstrate yet again her colossal lack of cleverness and urbanity in this new circumstance of passion. She would never bring herself to discuss it with the nonchalance of an Isabel, or even an Angela Lamb, reducing it to the commonplace or even rendering it a possible subject for humor. Her own love was still beautifully overpowering, like a wild summer lightning storm, and she was desperate to preserve the intensity with which every sight and sensation rolled over her. She began to crave this slight dizziness, this giddy abstraction which occurred when she contemplated Augusta's eyelids, teeth, and firm long wrist reposing on her side.

Augusta was speaking now; Sarah clung to each word, as she might have with strains of fine music, yet began to lose the thread of sense almost instantly. When Augusta paused for a reply, Sarah simply kissed her. Augusta responded first with startled mirth, then in kind. Sarah could not imagine anything closer to perfect contentment.

Augusta took her by the hand and pulled her

along more rapidly. The grounds were indeed damp from the previous night's showers, and Sarah felt the moisture seep into her boots.

"Almost there," Augusta promised. They had left the orchard and were entering a less cultivated area. A cluster of trees opened to reveal a charming brook, framed by rocks and bright green weeds. The water bubbled up, crystal white, between the huddled stalks. Augusta flung herself onto the largest rock, unbuttoned her boots, and tossed them up on the grass.

"This is my Eden," she announced, plunging her feet underwater and stretching out. "From now on, it can be ours. I'm going to bring you down here one day and paint a miniature of you, with the green grass as a background. Then you can make one of me, and we'll each have one to keep."

Sarah removed her own wet boots, found a place on the ground, and drew her knees up under her chin. "Edens can't last," she murmured.

"This one can. I know how I feel."

"As do I. But feelings themselves can be venomous sometimes."

Augusta climbed off the rock and threaded her way over. "I understand that you're afraid." She stroked the back of Sarah's hand. "But I have always done as I liked at Pym House, and there no one will judge us. We can live our lives celebrating the truth of ourselves, truth as we see and feel it, unencumbered by the willfully ignorant and their ravings. We can shape ourselves. I was nearly complete, before you. Now I can say that I am."

Augusta stopped, puzzled that Sarah looked stung to the bone by these words.

Sarah folded her arms over her knees and plunged her face into them. "You don't know the truth about me," she wept.

"What?" Augusta's face revealed her sudden panic. "What is it? A betrothal, an assumed name? Please, love! Don't drive me mad —"

Sarah shivered, and her chin came up. Augusta's earnest, seeking expression composed her somewhat. "You suppose me to be of impeccable background," she began, swallowing. "The fact is, my love, that I am not." She saw Augusta blink, totally uncomprehending. Sarah's story spun out in a torrent. She related the case just as Uncle Lionel had related it to her, omitting nothing and even tossing in a decidedly unflattering description of Mr. Hyde and his attentions to her at the birthday party. Augusta listened, brow creasing, her lips half-parted as though she were either mortified or on the brink of speaking. Sarah did not allow her to interrupt. Nor did she dare read her eyes.

"So you see," she finished hastily, "I am not the sort of person one could ever love safely. There are demons within me . . . of lust, and deceit. If all my other suitors knew it, and it left me unfit for even the likes of them, why shouldn't you, too, Augusta? You, who are so much more worthy than any of them."

"Well." Augusta twisted her fingers together, and stared at them in thought. "This certainly is quite a confession. But do you feel you could leave me like that, Sarah?"

"Oh, no, no! But I have little control over it, you see. Perhaps that was what brought last night on, as well. Perhaps I am incapable of real, honest love."

"Are you certain that was never what caused your mother to behave as she did?"

"How . . . how do you mean?" Sarah was pale. This question, amazingly, had never occurred to her.

"Perhaps it is really your Uncle Lionel who is incapable of knowing anything except lust. Perhaps the concept was beyond him that there is such a love for which one would forfeit even respectability, and blood? If so, it was certainly his loss. Don't you see that?"

"I . . . suppose it is no more than what I would gladly do for you, Augusta."

"Then that is her legacy to you, dearest." Augusta bent down and kissed the salty moisture from the younger woman's closed eyelids. "It is not shame, but your life. Although," she drew back in abrupt gravity, "it could present certain difficulties if we ever had children."

Sarah dipped her hand in the water and splashed her.

Toward early afternoon, when they returned to the house, one of the downstairs maids scurried down the marble steps to meet them.

"Yes?" Augusta asked, as if she sensed trouble.

"Oh, ma'am, it's Mr. Finch here to see you. He's been pacing in the morning room for close to an hour now, and he's terribly impatient. He does hope you can see him soon, ma'am. You and Miss Lindsay both."

"I can well imagine," sighed Augusta.

Sarah followed her up the steps, and as

Augusta's maid opened the terrace doors for them, Roderick Finch stepped out to meet them. He was smartly dressed and the physical effects of his personal excesses were today less apparent. He grinned with relief when he encountered them, his sunken cheeks lifting.

"Well, Lady Pym! How splendid you're back. I suspected you were when your little chit there went flying straight through the house to greet you. Feared I'd be trapped in that stuffy room until luncheon!"

"Oh?" Augusta offered a resigned but hospitable hand. She discreetly took it away when it seemed Roderick might kiss it. He settled for flashing a toothy smile at Sarah, who kept her arms at her sides. "You were of course free to have a window opened, Rod."

"Oh, pither." Roderick dismissed this idea with a fluttering motion. "An open window can't match the freshness of this fine countryside. Especially after a rain."

"We've just been enjoying it ourselves," Sarah said when he turned to her for approval.

"Were I of an artistic bent, I could make quite a use of dear Lady Pym's grounds."

"Would you care to walk back out with us?" Augusta politely inquired.

"Oh, but I almost forgot why I came. Isabel sent me." Roderick opened his striped tailcoat and produced small dove-gray envelopes. "One week from today, my sister plans to throw a luscious feast in celebration of Princess Drina's coming of age. Our future Queen won't be with us in body, of course, but Isabel claims she'll hear of it somehow. Thus are

133

royal favors culled, don't you know. Naturally, you'll both join us?"

"We'll be delighted."

"I overheard her discussing the menu with Cook. Grouse, China tea, French cream-cake . . ."

"Oh, Rod, don't finagle. Stay to lunch if you wish."

"Well, how kind!" Roderick acted as if this had never occurred to him. "Most pleasant to join you. And I should like to talk to you again, Miss Lindsay."

"We'll just go right in now, all right?" With a roll of her eyes, Augusta led the way.

Roderick clearly deemed himself a thorough success at luncheon. He entertained them for nearly an hour, or so he must have supposed, talking of horses and wagers and a new racing carriage Isabel had promised to buy him. As all the best conversationalists did, he touched on a variety of other topics, most of which were less repellant than intellectually deadening to Augusta and Sarah. Augusta, as the role of hostess obliged, suffered him with grace and patience, while Sarah stared at her wine glass and reflected that, for all her flaws of personality, Isabel was really the less painful of the two siblings to endure. Yet perhaps Roderick was his sister's creation, in a way. She had heard of her dotage already, and heard the proof of it in Roderick's own words.

At last he stood to go, pulling on a dainty pair of white gloves. "Well, Miss Lindsay, I shall see you at the dinner, if not before. Lady Pym, a lovely lunch. I should call every day could I hope to be so splendidly entertained."

"Dear Rod. We scarcely deserve such devotion. Tell Isabel we shall be delighted to dine with her."

Roderick glanced at Sarah as if he expected her to reply, too, but she simply smiled in her most subtly dismissive manner.

"Well, then." Roderick shrugged, and walked back to his waiting carriage.

"Lord," Augusta breathed as his vehicle left, and they both stifled laughter.

Later that evening, after Sarah had gone upstairs, Augusta sent for Lothaire. "You know I rely on your discretion, Madame," she said.

Lothaire nodded at once. "Yes, Lady Pym, of course."

"Well, then." Augusta took a sheet of paper, on which she wrote everything she knew about Lionel Lindsay: his home, and his parents. She underlined the name of Sarah's mother, then wrote a brief letter and stuffed both pages into an envelope. "This is to be sent to Mrs. Lillian Hamilton, in York. You remember her?"

"Yes, madam, very well."

"I am entrusting this letter to you personally. It concerns a matter of great personal importance to Miss Lindsay. I would trust no one but yourself to dispatch it."

"You can depend on me." Clutching her booty, Lothaire disappeared. Augusta capped the inkwell, and toyed with the pen. There had to be more to the matter of Miss Emilia Lindsay. If anyone could find out, it would be Lillian Hamilton. The woman's circle of acquaintances was larger than Dante's, and even more sly and knowing.

CHAPTER 9

The days immediately preceding the party at Isabel's house blew past in a hurricane of outdoor luncheons, endless garden walks, and scented evenings awash with more intense bodily pleasures. Augusta came to Sarah every night, as soon as the upstairs maids had retired, and each dawn left the tower room to await morning tea in her own. Only once had Sarah heard the rustle of skirts on the staircase and wondered if Augusta had been seen. But Augusta remained unconcerned. "It's still my house," she'd said to Sarah.

Since Augusta was resolved that they should appear quite the most fashionable guests at the Gerard's table, she arranged a visit to her own preferred tailor, tacitly ignoring Isabel's suggestion that they contact hers. "No mistaking her intentions there. We'll walk out wrapped in burlap." She'd smiled, and dashed off her own message the next morning. They were fitted for gowns complementary in both color and cut, then had ordered handkerchiefs and slippers to match.

They had returned home laden with purchases, and exhausted. Sarah had opened her own bundle to find hidden in the packaging an additional handkerchief embroidered with an interlocking A and S. Even now, seated at her dressing table with Valerie fussing around her, twisting her hair into shape for the party, she was fighting back a blush. This blush only deepened as she resisted it, for she remembered all too clearly what had followed this discovery. Augusta had anticipated the entire confrontation. Sarah scarcely had to engage her imagination at all to feel again the slither of garments as they dropped from her sides, Augusta's warm weight brushing over her instead, the flick of a moist tongue just beside her ear . . .

She caught her breath, and settled back with a smug expression. And society had always taught women that real passion was as alien to them as their brothers' classical readers!

"Oh, Miss, did I pull too hard?" Valerie froze, brush in hand, having misinterpreted her mistress's sudden gasp.

"No, no, you're doing just fine. Please continue."

138

"It's going to be a long night for you, I'll wager. I'm giving these curls some extra stay."

"Yes, a good idea." After the party, perhaps even in the carriage driving home, Augusta would lean over and rake her fingers through them, pull them back off her ears and neck, planting kisses on the places bared . . .

"And you'll be needing a diversion, I say," Valerie continued, missing the vacant expression of her audience. Sarah forced herself to pay attention. "Moping about all afternoon with a bunch of dirty old ledgers is no way to spend a visit, Miss. Like a proper pair of little old clerks, you and Lady Pym seem sometimes."

"Nonsense. Lady Pym is also teaching me painting and archery." The attempt at miniatures, of course, had proven a disappointment. Sarah, laughing at her own ridiculous effort to capture Augusta's shoulders and loose hair, had changed the shapeless blotch into a passable rock and turned out a tiny mediocre landscape. Augusta, having had the benefit of years of leisurely practice, had fared better.

"Well, if you're pleased, Miss, that's what matters most. I wondered, though . . ."

"Yes?"

"Well, Miss, whether or not we're still to go to Bath. We've been here weeks already, and the lady we were to see there might be getting into a pet and all. My mum used to not even open the doors to anyone who came late for a visit when they'd promised. Made my cousin Julia stand right in the downpour for an hour once, she did."

"Fortunately that shan't happen to us. On the contrary, we heard from Mrs. Waterbury just this morning. She's delighted that we met with Lady Pym, whom she knows by reputation, it seems, and has heard only good things of her hospitality. In fact, she's invited Lady Pym to join us, if she wishes to come. She'll make the arrangements once Lady Pym has replied. So, you see, we're in no hurry to leave now whatsoever."

It had helped, no doubt, that she had implied Uncle Lionel's consent to the whole escapade, Sarah mused. Without a doubt he would hear of the arrangement eventually, but she had no intention of rushing matters. Despite the good weather, letters could reach Uncle Lionel no sooner than a week or two after their dispatch.

To her surprise, Valerie's hand again paused, and Sarah heard her swallow as if to choke back a rash phrase she had instantly thought better of. Valerie settled for muttering in a subdued tone, "Lady Pym will be coming with us, then, when the time comes."

Sarah turned around in her seat. She saw the truth in Valerie's face at once. She and Augusta had been blind, she saw now, to suppose they could deceive all the servants except Madame Lothaire indefinitely. It didn't really matter at all which of them had noticed Augusta from the back staircase on that single occasion. What one maid knew was as good as public knowledge below-stairs.

"Valerie," she soothed, and reached out to cover the startled girl's wrist. "Valerie, do you judge me?"

"Oh, no, Miss, that's hardly my place . . ."

"Do you doubt Lady Pym's integrity? Or mine? I

can assure you on both counts that there is no need."

"No, Miss, I'm sure not." Valerie's voice had diminished to a strangled, humiliated whisper.

Sarah fought away a scowl of frustration. What other reaction had she any right to expect? How much tamer this one would be than most! Uncle Lionel's servant for one. Even Mrs. Waterbury's.

"Valerie, I will not say that I was not . . . confused, myself, when these things . . . came about. But Mrs. Lamb said something to me, something we must not, I think, doubt the truth and importance of." Sarah explained, as coolly as she could, and without the slightest condescension, Angela Lamb's theories on the inadvisability of defining human love. "Besides," she added smiling ruefully, "you would not prefer to see me bound to Mr. Ian Hyde for eternity?"

"Surely there are . . . surely you could meet some other, much finer gentlemen than him, Miss?"

"Perhaps I could . . . but it's still Lady Pym that I want. It shall always be her, Valerie, until God chooses to part my breath from my limbs. I have looked to my soul, Valerie, and I know this to be true, just as I know that I have not sinned in admitting this truth."

Their gazes locked, Valerie clearly not daring to contradict her again. Sarah was relieved not to read disgust or condemnation in that stare, but neither could she find real acceptance behind the clenched jaw and thin, rigid brows.

"If you choose to find another position, Valerie, I shall of course write you a very good letter, and provide your fare to any town you might wish. You need only ask me."

Slowly, Valerie brought the hairbrush back into service, but Sarah could sense that her mind was no longer on the party, and the final touches were accomplished in an atmosphere of crushing silence. Sarah's offer lingered like the scent of the water Valerie had liberally applied to her curls.

"I don't know, Miss," she said at last, biting her lip. "Truly I don't."

Isabel Gerard stood between her husband and brother in their high, polished foyer, and greeted her guests with immense satisfaction. The care with which they had adorned themselves bespoke their admiration for her, and cemented the importance of the gathering. Yet no one, whatever his or her intentions, had managed to outshine her. In the total patronage of both Sylvan and Roderick, she reposed in the soft glow of jewels and a teal gown cut low at the neck in the Grecian style that was causing a stir at all the fashionable parties in London. The guests, mostly titled, all of impeccable lineage, filed past her with a barrage of compliments, deferential kisses, and tributes. One gentleman in freshly curled hair and a full-shouldered waisted coat of amber velvet, declared that a single glimpse of her this evening would restore their ailing King William to perfect, lustful health. Isabel replied in great spirit that she hoped not, lest their purpose in gathering become quite muddled.

"Oh, I have admiration enough for our Princess

Drina," he laughed in reply, "though I cannot say King Will has treated us at all badly." Isabel knew he was referring to a peerage in his family, coaxed from the sovereign just that year. To mention the fact more specifically would have been unthinkable.

Isabel turned to her next arrivals, and found her gloved hand enclosing Sarah's. Augusta waited just behind her.

"Well, dearest," Isabel addressed Sarah for everyone to hear, "you shall certainly create a row tonight, as all the gentlemen clamor to sit round you."

Sarah inclined her head with respect. "No doubt our hostess endeavors to please everyone."

As they approached the threshold of the dining room, servants appeared to guide them to their seats. The table was set lavishly, each place aglow with highly polished silverware bearing Sylvan's initials, fragile wine glasses rimmed with gold, and copious bowls of freshly cut flowers. Sarah found herself placed between Roderick, who immediately rambled on again about horses, and a Mr. Redwell, who had once met her uncle. Augusta was on the same side of the table, closer to Isabel, between two older men she seemed to know well, and directly opposite Angela Lamb.

As the appetizer, fresh fish and thinly sliced potatoes smothered in white sauce, was handed around, discussion centered on the postulated future of Princess Victoria, whom some people continued to refer to as Drina. By the time the second course of game hens arrived, conversation had moved on to other, further-ranging topics such as King William's career and illness, long-term effects of the

Parliamentary reform he had imposed, and the origins and relative excellence of the various dishes served. Mr. Redwell could not help but compare Isabel's party with one he had recently attended near King Street in London, at the home of a Mrs. Harke.

"No contest, in fact," he remarked, shaking his head so that his cravat, fashioned of emerald silk and held in place with a tiny diamond, flashed in the candlelight. "She's one of these newfangled sorts, you know, refuses to serve meat of any kind, and I'm blamed if she didn't find several others of the same stamp to come and sit with us at table. Perfectly dreadful conversation, I needn't assure you, and not a few of her lilacs were actually wilted."

Sarah was forced to concede Mr. Redwell's extraordinary fortitude in emerging from such an ordeal unscathed.

"Yes, and one of the women was busy reading all this nonsense by a Miss Wollstonecraft. Surely you don't fancy all that rubbish about women rising up to overturn old England, and all that, do you, Miss Lindsay?"

"I hardly think that is likely to happen."

"Well, well, sensible of you. I didn't think your uncle was capable of raising a ninny."

"Thank you." Sarah half-turned from him and looked toward Augusta. Mr. Redwell's tall figure prevented her from obtaining a clear view, save for a brief glimpse of her slender hands and wrists as she reached for her wine glass or toyed with her cutlery. Dessert, a gigantic cake covered with cherries and a sugary glaze, was being pushed in on a wheeled cart by two maids. Only then did Augusta catch her eye, and the two of them managed to break free and exchange a few words and a fleeting but adequate smile. As Mr. Redwell again moved into position between them, Sarah saw Isabel Gerard nod to her.

She, Augusta, and Angela Lamb overstayed the other guests, sipping the remainder of the wine and sprawling in the plush seats of the sitting room.

"I hear from Rod that Sarah is putting her background to good use," Isabel said, rolling her slim-stemmed glass between her fingers. "Her financial background, I mean. Helping with the books or something, he said. So impatient to get back to them you barely stopped for tea."

"Rod called just as we were preparing the month's totals," Augusta explained. "My solicitors are due again in a few days, and I plan to have Sarah attend our discourse. They will badger me again to choose a new steward — someone of their recommendation, I'm sure. I plan to curb their impatience by displaying Sarah's wizardry. I can see their silly old faces now."

"I also understand you're uprooting all the cottagers. They can't be fond of that, as long as some of them have been sitting there virtually rent-free."

"We've reorganized a bit, true. But no one's been put out, and I've heard no complaints yet. When the solicitors get here it shall be another story."

"I am in no hurry to embarrass myself, Augusta," Sarah reminded her.

"Well and good, because you shall not." Augusta touched the younger woman's arm in sympathy.

Isabel, rolling the stem of her wine glass in her fingers, saw the simple gesture, saw the flash of approval in Angela's eyes. "The entertainments at Bath will be well underway now," she stated without the slightest emphasis in her voice.

After the party, Sylvan came to Isabel. She had known he would do so; this was her reward, her compensation for gracing his home and reputation with the perfect management of the party. She was writing by the window when he entered the bedroom, his tailcoat replaced by a dressing gown and his boots by Oriental slippers. He paused beside her writing table, hands behind his back. Her candle flickered between them, lifting the edges of the long rose-colored drapes hanging nearby.

"You're still going to London tomorrow, I assume?" she asked without turning around.

"Yes. I'll be away two days, as you know."

"You shall take some letters for me, then. They'll be delivered much more promptly if you carry them halfway."

"I shall be delighted." His hand crept along her shoulder.

"You did say Mr. Redwell could reach Mr. Lionel Lindsay?"

"I presume he can. Why would you wish to contact him? Surely Miss Lindsay —"

"This cannot be dispatched through Miss Lindsay. It would be too indelicate. You see, I am commending her to her uncle — telling him how much she has enriched our simple lives here and at Pym House, and how Augusta is so taken with the skills she learned at his knee that she's proclaiming her as her new steward!"

"That does sound like Augusta." Obviously charmed, he laughed at the absurdity of this.

Isabel did not laugh. "I think Augusta really would offer her employment if she supposed it would keep Miss Lindsay at Pym House through the season. What's more, I think the little fool would sign on as her parlor-maid to make it possible."

Sylvan's hand dropped away. "Why do Augusta's guests interest you so deeply? What can it matter to us how long Miss Lindsay stays? The woman has lost her husband. If this girl's society pleases her, and the girl is likewise content, what harm can come of it? Perhaps Lady Pym could even find her a match, superior to anything her uncle could offer."

Isabel smiled this time. "Of course Augusta shall always concern me. Silly Sylvan! If not for Augusta, I should never have met you." She picked up her letter. "Let me read what I've done so far."

Sylvan listened, lazily reading along as Isabel recited the expected lines praising Miss Lindsay's conversation, appearance, and breeding. The section detailing the jest about the stewardship was rather cleverly worded, Isabel felt, yet failed to elicit in Sylvan the same amusement it undoubtedly would in Lionel Lindsay.

"Very proper," he muttered when she asked his opinion. His fingers sought her shoulder, more insistently this time.

CHAPTER 10

The tiny parchment-colored calling card looked as though it were afloat in the center of the glimmering silver tray. One of the newer parlor-maids brought it into the salon. It lay face down in the tray's exact center.

"A gentleman, madam. I've left him in the morning room, as usual."

"Very well." Augusta turned the card over, read it, and replaced it without comment. Sarah had innocuously craned her head, but was unable to make out any of the tiny embossed letters. "We'll see him in here. Lay another place at luncheon, and be sure we have plenty of partridge. It's among Mr. Pearsall's favorites, as I recall."

"Mr. Pearsall?" Sarah pretended to return her attention to a sheaf of papers bearing monetary figures.

"A former member of our circle. A particular friend of Lewis's." Augusta kissed the frown on Sarah's forehead. "Bit of a sop, but likeable enough. He stops by every season, while he's on his way elsewhere. Be forewarned, he's on the melancholy side. Chooses his humors very carefully, I've always suspected."

Mr. Nichols Pearsall entered the room a few moments later. He was a small man, made to look smaller by the froth of coffee-colored ringlets hanging over his forehead and behind his ears. He wore a beautiful suit of indigo, offset by a pale yellow cravat held in place with a gold pin. He clasped Sarah's hand, kissed Augusta, and sank into a chair opposite them as if the simple act of greeting had exhausted him. He sighed. "Off to Rye for the summer," he explained. "Been at London, of course — the theatre."

"That ought to be very pleasant." Augusta steepled her fingers. "Have you seen anything of note on the stage?"

Mr. Pearsall rolled eyes that looked just a little too baleful. Sarah thought Augusta had been correct about his affectations. Augusta was really very astute about people.

"Oh, tosh. These melodramas are everywhere. Mournful little sailor boys mooning over overdressed coquettes, then discovering they're all the foundlings of noblemen. Mr. Jonson and Mr. Congreve cannot imagine how much they're missed."

"I understand the melodramas draw substantial crowds who would differ with you," Sarah put in. Augusta winked approval.

"The general populace of our England need not be encouraged in their philistinism. Anyhow, I've left all that behind. So, you've been at Pym House long, Miss Lindsay?"

"Rather long," Augusta answered for her. "I expect, Nichols, you would like to see the room again?"

"As always." He bowed his head in deference. "I shan't be stopping overnight, though."

"We'll be going in to luncheon soon. After that, I'll need to pay some calls on the cottagers. Miss Lindsay will escort you instead."

Those baleful eyes considered Sarah. "That is acceptable to me. You mustn't neglect your calls."

They dined together, pleasantly enough. Sarah found Mr. Pearsall quite intelligent, despite his initial demeanor, and his points about the decline of theatre were after all well-considered and in most cases valid. Sarah was, however, unsuccessful in determining the specifics of her after-luncheon assignment. What room was she to show Mr. Pearsall — surely not the salon, since he had been shown there directly — and to what purpose? Toward the end of the meal, to her relief, Augusta sent for Madame Lothaire, who came so promptly she could only have been waiting in the kitchen, perhaps taking her own meal in the cook's company.

"Yes, madam?"

"After lunch, I shall be visiting the cottagers to discuss the relocations we're considering, and the lessons for the children. While I am away, Miss Lindsay will be conducting Mr. Pearsall, whom you know, to Sir Lewis's room in the usual manner."

Madame Lothaire nodded. She smiled at Sarah, to her surprise. "Very good. They shall not be interrupted."

"Thank you." As Lothaire started to withdraw, she added, "We would all be quite lost without you here, you know."

"Yes, madam, sometimes I expect you would." Not bothering to suppress a further grin, Lothaire departed.

"She's your finest jewel, that one." Nichols pointed his chin at the swinging door.

"I would never joke about my staff. As I always say, we each have a function in this house, and depend on each other for no less than our lives. I value these people as I might my own family."

"Well, I keep no servants," Nichols stated emphatically, "but did I, I should quite see your point."

"Are we almost ready, then? I would like to stretch a bit. If the two of you would like coffee without me, simply ring and tell someone. I myself desire nothing more. We shall talk further when I return, Nichols."

"Of course." He rose as she left them, patting Augusta's shoulder as she swept past and out. When he dropped back into his seat, he faced Sarah with such blatant scrutiny she became uncomfortable all over again. "Lady Pym's regard for you is really very moving." He toyed with a spoon. "I hope you find her trust an honor."

"Really, Mr. Pearsall!" What business of his was anything that existed between herself and Augusta? She resented his intrusion, and in that moment she resented him. She and Augusta could have enjoyed a quiet luncheon to themselves, and, afterward, called on the cottagers together. The schoolroom scheme Augusta had mentioned to Lothaire had been mostly her own.

He must have sensed her irritation, for he opened his palm to her in supplication. "Please, I had no wish to offend you. Augusta and I, though, have few secrets from each other these days. When I have called in the past, she always accompanied me upstairs herself. Now . . ." He rose again. "I think perhaps we had better enjoy our coffee afterward. It is your place to order it, of course, if you so wish. Otherwise, I shall be pleased to ring." His hand paused above the bell.

Sarah started to defer to his suggestion, then thought better of it. He was right, of course, in a sense: Augusta was, in essence, yielding the duties of hostess to her. This was, indeed, a flattering responsibility. Abruptly she stood, too, and rang the bell. The serving-maid appeared, and Sarah gave the instructions regarding the coffee fully and courteously, in the very tone Augusta herself always used even when addressing her newest or youngest employees. Sarah had to admit that Uncle Lionel had never encouraged her to regard servants as important, or even human, in their own right. This blindness she attributed less to bigotry than to his own conditioning. At least it had not proven hereditary. Perhaps this was partially the reason that Valerie, very close-mouthed as of late, had not chosen to flee back to her former household.

"Yes, Miss Lindsay." The young woman ducked her head respectfully.

Sarah turned to Mr. Pearsall. No doubt his plans for Sir Lewis's room would become more apparent when they spoke further.

They trudged upstairs. Mr. Pearsall, not responding to her attempts to chatter, followed. She slowed her pace when they neared Sir Lewis's door, only proper in her opinion, but without warning Mr. Pearsall's composure slipped from his face. He grabbed for the knob, rushing in ahead of her, his cheeks flushing beneath the points of his silky whiskers. Once inside, he paced around and around, looking at things, touching the rings on the dresser, opening the wardrobe, smoothing the bedspread. Watching him, Sarah understood fully why he had come. Suddenly, the room had been filled with the aura of remembered love, the futile wanting she had found so significantly missing when she and Valerie had first broken in.

When he sat on the bed, collecting himself, and stared up at her, she too blushed. "You're embarrassed for my foolishness," he surmised. "In truth, so am I."

"I . . . think I understand how you feel."

"You never knew Lewis, I presume?"

"No."

He smiled. "I think you would have liked him."

"Actually, I think perhaps I would not have."

"Ah, you mean because of Augusta." Nichols Pearsall laughed. "No, no, we were all the dearest of friends. Lewis, Augusta, Isabel, and I. At one time we wondered if I ought not to marry Isabel. What a match that would have proven!"

"No doubt." Sarah pretended to straighten the objects on the dresser he had moved.

"A very civilized arrangement, though some might have labeled it otherwise."

"Have you called here, to see the room, when Isabel was with Augusta?"

"Once or twice, I think. Why?"

"Did Isabel ever take you up here, as I am doing now? Did Augusta ever suggest it?"

"No, and Isabel would never have offered. I'm not certain I'd have accepted. Sometimes I couldn't bear her tongue, brilliant though she is." He stood. "Now tell me something, Miss Lindsay. What will happen when you're forced to leave here? You are not a married woman, thus not your own mistress yet. Isabel was not, either, at the first. It all ended very badly, when she realized what that meant."

Sarah turned away from the dresser.

Pearsall nodded sympathetically. "You've put it out of your mind, as I expected. You can't be Lady Pym's guest forever, you know. You'll have to make plans."

"Since I've been here, I have taken every day as a gift. I . . . cannot think of leaving her."

"Don't leave her." Crossing the room, Pearsall gripped her hands in both of his and squeezed until the pain throbbed in her wrists as surely as it did in her throat and behind her moistening eyes. "For any reason. I was on my Grand Tour when Sir Lewis became ill. By the time I returned, he had been dead two weeks. I don't even know if he understood my last letter, though Augusta read it to him. Had I known, I would have walked halfway across Europe to reach him in time. I would have flung myself beside him, held him in my arms before everyone. What would I have cared then? Now I shall never hear his voice again, reading to me from some new volume just posted from London, or laughing . . ."

She pulled her hands free, and forced the tears down and away. "You needn't tell me these things, Mr. Pearsall. I can feel them for myself. Perhaps I have not had the years of experience you can claim, but I am well able to appreciate happiness now."

"Well, then!" He released her hands, and laughed again. "I see I needn't have worried. You are the one for Augusta, at that."

Augusta flew across the field, shaking her loosened hair into the wind, reaching up to secure her tall hat whenever her mount thundered over a particularly jagged patch of ground. She had just finished with her next-to-last group of cottagers and had taken quite a few notes in the tiny bound book she kept jammed in her hatband. The families themselves, all of whom she insisted be present when she sat down to discuss things in depth, were a good deal more knowledgeable concerning agricultural and estate matters than any of the city-based experts her solicitors periodically sent on inspections. Most of the cottagers, she had discovered, were willing to move to other areas of the property to better distribute work and responsibility. Augusta had written down their suggestions, voiced as often by wives and daughters as by their male counterparts, while all talked together in the kitchen.

The last family she had visited included the girl who would come to the house as a domestic the following season. Augusta had not been surprised to discover that she could barely read, even though she could write her own first and last name and add household figures accurately. Augusta had promptly added her to the list she was compiling at the back of the book, a list of potential pupils for the schoolroom Sarah had proposed earlier that week. Now, Augusta would no longer have to squeeze in various lessons given by herself, or assigned to one of her literate employees. Several times since Sarah had mentioned it, Augusta had caught herself plotting in too much detail the renovations to the cottage which they would use for this purpose. She had even allowed herself to imagine Sarah stocking a bookcase or directing the placement of a heavy desk.

Her mount slowed, and she refocused her attention in time to see another rider, obviously a man, approaching her with his cloak flapping behind him. Gradually, she guided her horse to a trot, and the other rider wheeled around to meet her. Roderick Finch's dull eyes blinked up at her.

"Hello, Augusta," he tipped his hat partway, then let it drop back over his eyes. "I'm just out taking a tramp. Lovely to run into you."

"You must have expected you would, though. After all, you're well inside my east boundary."

Roderick shrugged, dropped his head back, and opened his mouth rather ridiculously to take an extended breath. "I'm letting the birdsong wash over me lately," he explained. "So refreshing, don't you agree? Missed it, in the city. Actually, I thought you might be riding with Miss Lindsay. Wanted to pay my respects. Fine young woman. Excellent family, Isabel always says."

"Miss Lindsay is with a guest at the house. I had calls to perform . . ." Augusta's annoyance with Roderick provided a sudden inspiration. "And besides —" She toyed with her left glove. "I thought they might value the privacy."

Roderick's head came upright. "A guest? Not her uncle?"

"No. A young man, just arrived from London. He traveled all night, I expect, poor fellow. Hardly safe, but in these situations we must forgive a little foolhardiness."

"Indeed." Roderick fidgeted in his saddle as though his posterior were hurting him, and his blotchy cheeks puckered with confusion. He wiped at his upper lip. "Well, I trust Miss Lindsay would never suffer a fool. Hardly the sort she's been brought up to admire, Uncle Lindsay being such a sensible fellow."

"I couldn't say." Augusta leaned down to stroke her mount's burly neck. "I haven't met Mr. Lindsay myself."

"Oh, Isabel's formed a rather extensive opinion of his character already. She claims that what one omits in a letter is often just as telling as what one includes."

Augusta's hand dropped. "In a letter? What do you mean by that, Rod?"

Not listening, he rambled on. "She's always claimed, too, that she can judge a chap by his handwriting. You know, tell one everything about him just from the way he slants his *g*'s and slashes his *t*'s. Bunch of pither, I say, but why puncture her fancies? Never listens to me, anyhow."

"Rod," Augusta stared at him, dumbfounded, "where has Isabel ever seen Mr. Lindsay's handwriting?"

"Well, she wrote to him of course." Roderick blinked. "Thought she would've told you. Invited him to come and join Miss Lindsay, asked him to stay with us if you hadn't the space. Kind of her, don't you think? Course, I half expect she did it for me. Meet the family, you know, so as not to say something out of turn or what have you . . ." He bent forward in his saddle. "God's blood, Augusta, you're looking green. Lothaire been bottling her own beer, or something?"

"Go up to the house, Rod," Augusta stuttered, her lips numb. The reins nearly slipped from her fingers. "Pay your respects to Miss Lindsay. I must be about my own calls now." Before he replied, she whipped around and galloped off. Her mount kicked a cloud of brown dust up between them.

Augusta blew through Isabel's front door like a summer storm through Dover. She ignored Janet, who reached for her cloak, and barged instead into Isabel's study unannounced. No one. She moved to the parlor. Janet, startled, followed her mouthing words she did not hear. Thwarted by the morning room, Augusta lost patience. "Where is Mrs. Gerard?" she half-shouted.

"I'm right here, dear Augusta," Isabel answered sweetly. She appeared on the stairs in a new gown and fresh coiffure. Augusta's own forehead was dripping.

"Rod," she breathed, charging for Isabel, "Rod told me about your damned letters."

"Oh?" Isabel threw back her head. "Silly Rod. I had no idea he was even paying attention to such things. Anyway, it's no secret. I can write to whomever I wish, can't I?"

Augusta wrenched Isabel's wrist. Isabel gasped, then clenched her teeth. "What, in God's name, did you tell the man?" Augusta hissed.

"Nothing you wouldn't yourself. And you really should have written, Augusta, by all the rules of decency. I can't imagine why you didn't. Then again, perhaps I can."

"Why would you do such a thing, Isabel? Why interfere, when you knew how I felt —"

"God's blood, Gussie, mind the servants! Now, enough wild tussling on the steps. Come upstairs and converse like a lady."

Furious, Augusta followed Isabel up to her bedroom. In this room Augusta felt her shoulders stiffen, to which Isabel lifted a brow. "Oh, really, Augusta, we've no unseemly memories here."

"How dare you say that to me? Now tell me about these letters, Isabel."

Isabel gestured toward her writing-desk. "They're over there someplace, dearest. You can read them in full if you like. As I told you, I mentioned nothing amiss. Only how much we all enjoyed Sarah's fine company and hoped she'd be with us for some time . . ."

"You want to ruin my happiness. Isabel, I'd not have believed it of you!"

"Oh, Augusta, what would you have me say? That I thought I could bear to see you together, but find that I cannot? That I wish to return to things as they were seven years ago? That I've taken religion, and am burning in trepidation for your soul? If you want that, I shall gladly say it. But you would still not know the truth."

"Well, tell me the truth, then!" Augusta shook her. They stood frozen for several moments in a configuration that seemed oddly like a half-embrace. She pulled away.

Isabel swallowed. "I am making you face the inevitable, dearest. You have Miss Lindsay now, and I've no doubt she's an exemplary . . . guest. Still, she'll never stay with you forever. How could she? She hasn't the freedom, any more than I had. She will marry, and be gone. She isn't like us, Augusta. You know that."

"She is very much like you, you mean."

"I toyed with inviting Uncle Lionel to the banquet, you know. But in the end I decided I'd

160

spent so much time preparing for it I couldn't bear to see it spoiled."

"Is Mr. Lindsay coming, then?"

"Not here. He's already refused. But you'll be hearing from him again, I've no doubt."

"And I shall have to put him up myself?"

"Well, of course you needn't offer. He'd never suggest it! I can see why it would be impractical, though. Are you and Miss Lindsay still in separate rooms? As we always were? I'd sneak out of the tower room just after dark . . . Madame Lothaire would bring me a candle sometimes . . ."

"I haven't forgotten. But it cannot matter now, Isabel."

"No? It's never ceased to matter to me, Augusta."

"I'm going. Sometimes I do thank whatever God there is that you left me, Isabel, no matter what I may have felt once." She took hold of the knob.

Isabel shrugged. "In my own way, you know, I really am sorry."

Augusta shook her head bitterly and opened the door. They both stopped. Sylvan was there, staring glassy-eyed into the room, his face pale white and moist with sweat. His arms hung rigid by his sides, and his hands, balled into fists, were shaking.

Sarah and Mr. Pearsall endured Roderick Finch's company for more than half an hour before the sounds of a carriage and at least two horses in the circular drive distracted them. They had been walking in the rear gardens, and hurried around to the front to see a large number of maids scurrying about, one of them even carrying a folded wet cloth. Sarah was reminded of the day she'd arrived.

"God's blood, Roderick drawled, open-mouthed, "that's one of our gigs."

A group of maids parted and Sarah spotted Augusta. Apparently she was supervising them as they aided someone out of the carriage. An unseen woman was barking that they were handling her too roughly. Finally Isabel's head surfaced, and she came down the steps with a kitchen girl on either side of her. Sarah was astonished when she saw her face.

Valerie had run up beside Sarah when Mr. Pearsall had gone forward to help. "Oh, Miss, did you hear? Betsy says there's been a terrible row between Mrs. Gerard and her husband! Lady Pym was there to see it, she says! Oh, Miss, and look at the bruise! He might have killed her, if she'd been alone . . ."

Isabel was being carted past Sarah even as Valerie spoke. A long purple bruise, which in truth did not look as though it could have been caused by a hand, ran the length of her jawbone. Isabel's eyes met Sarah's, and the uninjured half of her mouth twisted into a smile.

"The tower room," she announced to the servants supporting her. "I wish to be put in the tower room."

CHAPTER 11

In the end, fortunately for whatever vestiges of household peace remained, Isabel allowed herself to be taken to the Green Room, which Augusta had hastily touted as much more soothing to the nerves in terms of both structure and color. Besides, the smell of lilacs freely wafted through the windows and was especially potent in the evenings. Isabel demanded, in return for this large concession, that cool bandages be wrapped around her bruised jaw, and these bandages checked and changed ever twenty minutes precisely. Augusta duly assigned

163

Betsy to take complete charge of Pym House's latest arrival. By some miraculous intervention, Isabel found Betsy quite agreeable and possessed of sympathetic eyes. Not at all like her own servants, Isabel emphasized, who were eager to scalp her or at least burn her tongue mute with boiling tea every morning, evening, and afternoon.

Sarah stayed in the salon most of that afternoon, watching the endless procession of linen, restorative spirits, and even freshly cut flowers paraded upstairs by Betsy and a variety of helpmeets. Even Mr. Pearsall put off his leaving for a few hours and went upstairs to enjoy a private conversation with the patient which lasted almost forty minutes. Roderick Finch, too, had decided to extend his visit, and wandered from room to room lamenting his sister's confinement and denouncing Sylvan's brutality.

"For heaven's sake," Augusta exploded at one point, "I told you, Rod, it wasn't anything like that. She fell against the wardrobe. It's true that Sylvan shook her —"

"Just as barbaric!" Roderick wailed back. "No domestic peace at all any longer! What's this country coming to? I should sooner shoot myself than treat my own wife that way!" At this juncture his gaze fluttered meaningfully upon Sarah. She had reached, by now, the breaking point, and fled to the garden.

Augusta joined her a bit later. "Sent him off for some brandy. Luckily Isabel has it in her room. He is flesh of her flesh, after all, so let her deal with him."

Sarah's hand had been poised over a cluster of pale yellow buds and curved pointed leaves. She brought it away roughly, knocking some of the buds loose. "Isabel likes it here," she snapped. "She's grateful it happened — whatever did, really. You haven't stood in one place long enough even to tell me."

"Sylvan overheard some bits of a conversation he should not have."

"That much even Rod gathered."

"Well, it's quite true he went into a rage. He started for me first, then wisely thought better of that and turned to Isabel. She tried to slap his hands away and in the process turned straight into the wardrobe door. Blamed her servants for that, too, of course, a moment before she collapsed. Going to take Sylvan to the magistrate for attempted murder, she swears. He's convinced I'll back her up. It's clear to him, he says, that I don't care a whit for my own reputation. Might as well revel when his is destroyed, too." She tapped her chin in mock thoughtfulness. "Mind, he does have something."

"It couldn't have worked out better for her. She's left him . . . and come straight to you."

"She's come to my *house*," Augusta emphasized.

Sarah sensed that she was about to grasp her shoulders, and subtly moved away.

"And I'm not glad, Sarah, I swear it. But what could I do? How could I not offer her hospitality, when the incident was my doing?"

"Isabel is hardly without resource."

"Give her a few days. Angela Lamb will come to fetch her, mark my words."

"A few days, a few nights." Sarah spiraled her fingers upwards in the air. "What of it, that's nothing!"

165

This time Augusta did seize her. "Isabel has no claim on my nights."

"She did once," Sarah whispered. "And besides, what of Uncle Lionel? When he arrives to fetch me — and he will — what then?"

"Why are you asking me that, love? You're the one who will have to decide then."

"What can you mean by that? I've no decision to make. I've already told you my place is here with you. I believe that. I won't leave Pym House . . . unless you wish me to, of course."

"Don't launch toy arrows at me, Sarah — it's beneath you, you know." Augusta's grip on her arm tightened.

Sarah's anger gradually ebbed, and, still shaky, she pressed against Augusta's sturdy frame. Her cheek nestled in the solid crook of Augusta's shoulder.

"We could leave for Mrs. Waterbury's before he arrives," Augusta said tentatively.

"Run from him, you mean?" Sarah pulled away, settling back on her own heels. "Foolish, really. He'd only follow us there, wouldn't he, and make his sordid accusations in front of her. He hides little from her. They're very old friends."

"He'll have few accusations to make. He doesn't know any details. To that extent, I believe Isabel."

"Why should we trust her? How can you, after this? And after everything else."

"Oh, in her way, Isabel is trustworthy. Or at any rate predictable. She knows she'd have nothing to gain by proving me immoral and debauched. Her own proximity to me, after all, is the foundation of her social standing. She knows that."

"I know myself what it is to draw strength from you." Sarah pulled Augusta close to her. They stood for a moment, watching the bright buds around them stir in a faint breeze. They tipped their foreheads until they just touched.

"For now, I think we should work on getting that bruise off her cheekbone. Once we do that, we'll be dealing with a different Isabel."

"Well, I can't go back there, surely you see that." Roderick hurled himself around the study as Augusta checked the evening menu, brought to her by a boy from the kitchen. She didn't bother to look up. "The man is a lunatic. He'd probably challenge me with his old war sword, or something."

"I'm the one he'd prefer to run through," Augusta said.

Roderick paid no attention. He clutched his hair and arched his spine like something from Mr. Hogarth's tableaux. "Yes, by God, that's it! He means to murder me! I could give evidence, he knows, that he treated her coldly, that he was addicted to drink . . . Goodness knows what else she expects me to say!"

"Perhaps you ought to go and ask her. You might add, too, that you don't intend to reveal anything but the truth. A sentence for perjury could be far worse than enduring Sylvan's wrath."

"Well, I can't go to her. She's thrown me out yet again. Oh, Gussie, surely you have another room for me? I'd only stay the night, until I could send somewhere to procure another invitation. Besides, I ought to be with her at this terrible time. Family falling apart . . . tossed from our own home . . ."

"Augusta," Nichols Pearsall thankfully interrupted. He and Sarah had just entered the study, Nichols in his riding gear. "I'm afraid I've come to pay my farewells. I've just seen Isabel, and commend her to your care. Will you see me off?"

"Leaving already?" Roderick brightened; Augusta saw straight through his assumption that another guest room was now vacant. "Well, we are sorry to see you go."

"A shame you're not going on to Rye as well, Roderick." Augusta flashed an innocent smile at both men. "Mr. Pearsall could have accompanied you."

"Well, never know, never know." Roderick shrugged, while Mr. Pearsall darted a murderous grin at Augusta. "Maybe one day."

"I look forward to it," Nichols said. He walked to the foyer with Sarah and Augusta. Roderick occupied himself with the menu.

"Perhaps we shall meet in the autumn," Nichols held one hand to either of them. "All three of us, of course."

"Yes," Augusta pressed his hand.

Sarah did the same, and with genuine affection. In this man's frank eyes she began to see some hope for the situation after all. She recalled his willingness to declare himself in front of everyone in Sir Lewis's crowded death-chamber, and knew that little less would soon be required of her. Yet her own confession would not echo from the depths of a half-open tomb, but a bright jeweled box in which lay the future.

After he left them, she stood very still by the

staircase. "It's time, you know," she told Augusta. "Time I went to speak to Isabel."

Augusta did not seem surprised. Instead, she kissed Sarah's fingers and let her hand drop. Sarah said nothing further, but plodded up the stairs and wound her way down the long hall to the Green Room.

Isabel was sitting up, propped by at least four pillows, holding yet another cup of tea in both hands. Her bruise was covered by the damp bandage, but a tiny stain, livid purple, poked out just below her cheekbone.

She set the teacup down with a clink when she saw Sarah. "Well, Miss Lindsay! High time you came to visit me in my infirmity. Between Rod and the languishing Mr. Pearsall I thought I really would die. Do sit."

Sarah took the chair angled towards the bed and moved it closer. "You're looking better, Isabel."

"I suspect this is what childbed must be like. Not that I shall ever know firsthand, of course." She winked at Sarah.

"And in all likelihood I shan't either. So we have no way to verify your observation. Pity it will go to waste."

"Well, dearest, let us wait and see about that." The half of Isabel's mouth not restricted by the bandage curved into a strange smirk.

"Time will never move backwards for you, Isabel." Sarah knew any preamble would be useless now; instead she placed her hands firmly on the chair-arms, and held her face perfectly still as she spoke. "We shall never live those days again. In my case I should sooner die than go back to what I was

169

before Augusta. Fortunately, it is beyond your power to force me."

A cloud seemed to pass over Isabel. The scent of the lilacs, unusually powerful just then, permeated the room, and she floundered against her pillows in an effort to raise herself to Sarah's eye-level. "I have never forced anyone to do anything. Surely you see that. You're an intelligent girl. People do things for me because they wish to. Even Augusta. I didn't ask her to bring me here now. She isn't even angry any longer."

"You will always be her closest friend." Sarah swallowed even as she said it. "I would not think of preventing that. Even I could be your friend."

"You're not angry either." Isabel sniffed, as if in triumph, and sank back into comfort again. "You see the inevitability of it."

"I saw the inevitability of your husband putting you out, I suppose, even as you did. And I see the inevitability of Augusta doing the same."

"Because you intend to make her? Oh, really."

"On the contrary, because you shall. Then you shall move on to someone else, and then do the same again. I'm surprised you can't see it yourself."

"Oh, you silly child! Can you really love Augusta, and yet be so simple? I have no intention of returning anywhere but to my own home. You think Sylvan won't have me? Royal bosh, as my brother would snort. He'll be here any time to ask Augusta if he can see me. I won't let him, of course. Not at first. But eventually he'll persuade me, and I shall cast my eyes to the floor, smiling, and compliment his understanding, and he shall load half my things with his own hands and drive me back across the field, promising me trips to London and the Continent the entire time. Let us see whose portrait is the more accurate!"

"What he knows of you will curb his admiration, I think."

"Because he knows I loved Augusta? Nonsense, he's half accused me of that a hundred times anyhow. Oh, his little prideful soul will throb a bit, but in the end he'll convince himself it was a shrouded blessing. It would have been far worse for me had it been Sir Lewis I had loved. Now, there's a fancy for you." Isabel paused a moment, staring into space as if to conjure just such a ridiculous image, and sputtered at it.

Finally she faced Sarah again. "You don't realize it yet, as I didn't, but that is the way these matches must remain. One running ahead, one flying along to catch up. You see, that is why you are quite wrong for Augusta. You are the one who ought to be running ahead, but you'll always lag behind Augusta. You could do that, with a man. They usually aren't bright enough to see it, like poor Sylvan. Yet listen to him boasting, some night after he woos me back."

A long silence stretched between them. Isabel pulled her tea-tray to her knees. "I'm going to call Betsy back, to take these things away. You ought to go now. Augusta will be ringing the supper-bell, anyhow."

"Perhaps that would be best." Sarah got up, smoothing her skirts. Her spine felt cold, her elbows stiff. She had been clutching the chair-arms harder than she'd realized.

Yet Isabel's words had, on the whole, failed to offend her. What remained with her instead was not really pity, but an utter detachment. Isabel's world, she now knew, co-existed with hers only insofar as they shared the bright scent of the lilacs below, the sound of the teacup rattling on its tray, the soothing paint on Augusta's high walls.

Yet they were actually like two tiny dolls Sarah had owned as a child. Both dolls were positioned in a fine big dollhouse Uncle Lionel had had sent from France. The larger doll had been placed by the fire, her little satin skirt-hem stretching over the hearth-rug toward the grate. The smaller one, whose painted eyes differed in size, had reclined on a sofa with a miniature page of sheet music, dropped and forgotten, at her feet. But it was only this doll who could look up and out of the dollhouse's non-existent roof, right into Sarah's face and Lionel's big parlor which had become a nursery. The bigger doll saw nothing but the paper flames inside the wooden fireplace. Sarah had seldom moved her; she had been happy there, she knew, content to be left undisturbed by the large clumsy hands that periodically intruded to rearrange her furniture.

"I do love Augusta, you know," she stated before stepping out again.

"Now your Uncle Lionel will be very pleased to hear that," replied Isabel.

By the time dinner convened, Augusta had succeeded in packing Roderick off to the nearest pub, having even provided a small donation to accomplish her objective. The dressed mutton and potatoes had just been placed on the table when they heard a commotion outside the dining room doors.

"My business with Lady Pym is of the utmost urgency," a man's voice was insisting. "No, I would not care to wait."

Augusta set down her wine as the door heaved open and Sylvan Gerard stumbled in toward them. He blinked behind his spectacles, as if he had disbelieved the maid outside and not expected to find them at dinner at all.

"I . . . apologize for the impropriety of this intrusion, Augusta."

"I'd say we're a pace beyond strict propriety anyhow, Sylvan. Perhaps you'd care to join us?" Augusta spread her hand over the table. Sylvan swallowed, and eyed Sarah with nervous distaste. "Do forgive us if we don't break off in the middle of our meal, but the day has been rather hectic and we value the opportunity for leisure."

"Yes, well . . . well, I shan't keep you long. I came to see Isabel, really. She's not dining with you, then?"

"She, too, was anxious for privacy. She's upstairs . . . indisposed, as you know."

Sylvan's cheeks flushed. He lifted his hands, palms outward, and his voice sounded high and frightened. "Upon my soul's eternal torment, Augusta, I never meant to do it! Surely you can imagine my own pain! Not that I expect you to sympathize."

"Oh, Sylvan, don't behave like Rod. That would

be as repulsive as if you'd come back to claim her by force, hauling six feet of rope behind you and three workmen."

"I wouldn't have done that." Sylvan's nostrils flared. "You are not so very bitter, are you, Augusta, because it was finally me she chose? I didn't force her then, either."

"It's immaterial now." Augusta speared a chunk of meat and popped it in her mouth.

"Even then, you saw the need. You yourself were married. I wondered . . . did Sir Lewis know?"

"Yes, he did."

"Well, I see he conducted himself as a reasonable man ought. I respect that, and in honor of his memory I am prepared to do likewise."

"How very noble, Sylvan."

"After all, I have two younger sisters. I know what these affections between girls can be. In fact I have always considered them very charming, so long as innocence is not irretrievably lost." He spun around to Sarah. "Do you not agree, Miss Lindsay?"

"No doubt some would define innocence differently than you, Mr. Gerard."

"Well, Sylvan, my evenings of ethical discussions ended when we disbanded the salon," Augusta said. "If you wish to see her . . ."

"Before I do, I have one further question. Was Isabel . . . faithful to me, after the actual marriage?"

"As far as I was concerned, you mean?" Augusta fixed him with a stare of absolute contempt.

Sylvan flushed all over again, his sedate righteousness evaporating. "Well, er . . . yes."

"In that case, the answer is yes. Even though I could not understand her decision at the time, and

174

frankly I sometimes still cannot, I was never willing to share her. I needn't have. I need not now."

"At least you value honor to that degree. Isabel is not like you, you see. She is well beyond the pale of the ordinary. I knew that fact when I first spoke to her, in this very house. Such people must have a shield they can carry before them when they wade among the common herd. For a time, you were that shield. Now, I am."

Augusta nodded, and raised her glass to Sarah. "You certainly kept her from harm this afternoon, Sylvan."

"I've already explained that! We all lost our tempers. But really, I believe I've concluded my business with you. I want to see her."

Augusta rang the bell. A maid appeared. "Mr. Gerard wishes to visit his wife. Send someone upstairs, will you please, and see if she consents?"

"Will you not accompany me? Or Miss Lindsay?"

"As I told you, Miss Lindsay and I are at dinner." Augusta then initiated a conversation involving the rear garden, to which she planned to introduce a sculpture. Angela Lamb would no doubt be able to recommend something.

Sylvan wandered the length of the room, finally leaning on one arm against the china cabinet. "I'll tell you what I'm planning," he said. "That Isabel and I go to France for a year, two if it pleases her. Or Italy, if she prefers it."

Betsy herself entered then. "Mrs. Gerard sends her regrets, sir." She curtsied casually. "She is still unwell and cannot entertain just now."

"I don't wish to be entertained! She is my wife —"

"Sylvan," Augusta broke in sternly, "you really are losing my good will. If she cannot see you, your visit is over."

"No. I shall write to her. May I use your study, Augusta?"

"Betsy, show Mr. Gerard to the study. Stay with him while he writes, then send someone else up with the letter and wait for a reply. If none is forthcoming, show Mr. Gerard out."

"Yes, ma'am. If you'll please come this way, sir?" Betsy held the door open. With a wounded expression, Sylvan slunk out.

Sarah carved her meat in silence. "Augusta?"

"Yes, love?"

"Did he mean to injure her face?"

"Good God." Augusta pushed her plate back, settled against her chair, and studied the tablecloth. "Who can say?"

Sarah did not wait for Augusta to steal to the tower room that night; she went to Augusta's. In the hazy light of a single candle, the single sheet covering them felt like the dark velvet lining in the jeweled box she'd envisioned in Isabel's room. Augusta's head was at her breast, her nails idly tracing patterns on Sarah's middle.

"If you've any thought of leaving, you know, you'd better go off with Uncle Lionel. It would hurt me less, in the end."

"No. Not with Uncle Lionel, not ever."

"Such words come all too easily in situations like this."

"Isabel used them?"

"Yes. The day she left here, I ran through every room, through every hallway, screaming every curse word — excepting those she'd taught me, of course. Then I walked up and down the main staircase close to seventy times, until my legs gave out under me. I wouldn't let Lothaire lift me up, and so I slept there, on the middle step, half the night. The other half I spent in the study, with my head on the desk. I never want to feel that kind of agony again. I never asked Isabel if she felt anything similar. A laughing new bride, being led through her husband's home . . . I doubt it."

Sarah stroked Augusta's ear. Augusta closed her eyes and began to lapse into sleep. Sarah whispered, "I'll never be like her. I'll even tell everyone, starting with Uncle Lionel. I'd prefer it if he didn't want me back."

"You flatter me, love, but it can't be that way. The real test for us must be not how open we can be, but how secretive. Even in our own home, here, we can't always do as we please. There will always be occasions when we'll have to fall back on the only England we have."

"The one controlled by the Sylvan Gerards, you mean."

"Do you know of another? Please tell me, if you do, and I shall spirit you away there posthaste."

Sarah knew she had no possible reply, so instead she mused about the day when a Queen Regent would ascend the steps of Parliament for the first time in over two hundred years. King William was failing further every day, and Drina had now attained her majority. Not that they could hope for

177

much change at first, maybe not for any at all. But the most jaded male eyes in the kingdom would now be forced to seek sovereign approbation in a quick, strong-willed young woman who had not even been born the daughter of a king. She would sweep through her chambers in the mornings to find them kneeling to her when she emerged.

Sarah liked that image, and drifted away as she elaborated the details of the Queen's firm, intelligent expression and the embroidery on her lace-fringed bodice. The Queen passed beyond the kneeling courtiers and into a room filled with dancers, all of whom seemed to be women. Sarah herself was soon in the midst of them, floating alone through the swirl of brightly dyed dresses and unbound long hair. At first she was astonished to perceive herself, apparently detached, standing before the French windows gesturing. As she moved closer, however, she realized that this would have been impossible. The soft ruddy face before her was her mother's. Sarah paused next to her, uncertain.

"The garden is lovely," her mother told her, turning to peer out past the long curtains. This was certainly true; even the unpaved pathway was studded with plump ruby buds and plush purple stems that dragged on the tall grass. Augusta was walking by some willow trees, absorbed in her own thoughts.

"Yes." Sarah nodded, watching Augusta.

"I have grown everything in it with my own hands," her mother informed her proudly, and displayed her long fingers, none of which were encumbered by rings, like those of almost everyone else present. "When I am gone, Sarah, I shall leave its cultivation and upkeep entirely to your wits." Her hands clasped Sarah's. Her skin was very warm, almost feverish. "It shall be my legacy."

A light rain had begun to fall in the garden. Augusta hurried up the path, holding her arms over her hair, and dashed up the steps into the ballroom. Sarah's mother stepped away, and merged again with the other guests.

"Getting rather cool out there," Augusta said, shaking off water.

"No matter," Sarah said, embracing her. "We can stay right here."

Late the next morning, two events of importance occurred. First, Isabel descended for breakfast, informed them that Sylvan had already called and left another note, and that she would be returning home just before luncheon. The following month they would leave for the Continent, and she went so far as to invite Sarah to visit them there.

"You, dear, won't be welcome for a while, I fear," she said playfully to Augusta.

The second event took place not long after her gig, filled with borrowed pillows, had rolled out of the drive. They received a letter, actually addressed to Augusta, which informed them that Mr. Lionel Lindsay would be arriving at Pym House within the space of three or four days, if the weather permitted.

CHAPTER 12

The early afternoon sun had only partially dried the scattered puddles of dark, cool water left by the previous day's torrents. The gravel on the circular drive was damp, too, and failed to crunch properly beneath Lionel Lindsay's Italian boots as he stepped down from the chaise and strode toward the front entrance. The house's façade, impressive as it may have been from an architectural standpoint, also seemed to him soggy and lifeless — anemic, somehow, perhaps a result of years of withstanding similar assaults of the climate. Still, its size and well-sculpted grounds, despite a few broken branches and torn leaves which lay scattered at his feet, spoke of valued lineage and a good sense of a property's worth, much to his personal relief and professional satisfaction.

He stood for a moment, scanning the windows of Pym House with critical eyes, then shifted his walking-stick to his left hand and marched up to take hold of the ornate knocker. A smallish downstairs maid responded almost immediately.

"Please inform your mistress that Mr. Lionel Lindsay has arrived — by appointment." After handing her his tall hat and overcoat, Lionel produced his card. With what he considered more than adequate deference, he was escorted to a very pleasant sitting room, furnished with several periodicals and tasteful works of art to amuse the waiting caller.

He chose neither to read nor to observe, but took a seat on a plush settee and crossed his wrists over his knee. He listened as the maid's footsteps receded down the hall. Presently he heard a door open and close, and then was forced to endure a long silence. Lionel pursed his lips and continued to sit motionless.

The same maid returned. Lionel rose immediately, but first smoothed the front of his waistcoat and dashed a speck from his dark striped trousers.

The maid bobbed with respect. "Lady Pym is delighted to receive you, Mr. Lindsay. If it would please you to come with me, your niece asks you to join her for tea in the parlor. Her ladyship will be with you both directly."

"That is acceptable to me." Lionel followed her across the glistening foyer and to a set of rooms nestled at the far side of the ground floor. A set of polished double doors stood open to receive him.

As he entered, Sarah stood from behind an impressive tea service. Lionel stared at her rich garments, none he had ever noticed her wearing before, and her demure, almost icy smile. A stranger, entering the house as a first-time caller, might actually have supposed her to be Lady Pym herself.

"Sarah," he said, as soon as the servant had left them alone.

Sarah gestured to the sofa placed opposite hers. "Welcome to Pym House at last, Uncle. Will you sit? Your tea has already been poured."

Lionel looked down to find that this was so. Sarah picked up her own cup, settling herself again without a moment's awkwardness. "We feared the rain might detain you."

"Not at all. I was determined to keep my word."

"And you have. As I said before, Uncle, welcome."

Lionel lifted his cup, then jerked it away again without tasting his tea. The heated words he had rehearsed all morning in the final leg of his carriage journey suddenly seemed ludicrous, wholly inappropriate in this genteel setting. He suspected Sarah knew that. She knew him too well. This entire interview had been calculated. Spots of heat erupted at the tips of his whiskers.

"Now, really, Sarah, this Mrs. Gerard's letter — the insinuations she has made I cannot dismiss! You serving as some gentlewoman's steward, behaving as though you were some salaried lackey! Things could scarcely be more disgraceful if you'd signed on as someone's governess! Have you no sense of maintaining position, of increasing your personal respectability? Good heavens, Sarah! Have you rejected me to so great an extent already?" His fingers were pressed white against the sides of his teacup; he felt the beginnings of heat blisters, and banged it down on the tray with a gasp.

Sarah, still sipping at her own, regarded him as though he had just deposited its full contents in his lap. "Uncle, my goodness! Do be careful. Lady Pym only tolerates hot tea to be served in her home. Too often, she says, we must make do with the merely lukewarm, and I must agree with her that this is far more acceptable."

"I am not interested in tea, Sarah! Have you no answer for me, then? No defense at all? I thought as much."

"Actually, I had every intention of responding, but the fact that you were about to be burned alarmed me. My mistake; now I recall you prefer hot tea yourself. Well, in any case, Uncle, I'm quite surprised that you have taken Mrs. Gerard's letter so literally. Of course, she and Lady Pym are great friends, and often indulge in the most spirited conversations. I suppose it simply didn't occur to her that her particular species of wit would prove misleading to someone not regularly in contact with her. She would be most amused by your reaction, though, I am certain."

"Then you are not working for this woman? You have not accepted money from her, under any pretext?"

"I have accepted her hospitality, and her most sincere overtures of friendship." Sarah freshened her tea, lowering her head to conceal a smirk. "We met while traveling, as Mrs. Gerard must have told you."

"Yes, yes, she did. You were due at Mrs. Waterbury's more than three weeks ago, in fact! Why was I not informed until now, and by a complete stranger? I cannot help but think you have been concealing your whereabouts for some ulterior purpose."

"But I did send a letter!" Sarah blinked up at him with all the innocence of a new-born kitten. "Did you not receive it?"

"I received no letter," he stated.

"Well, that is hardly my fault, is it? The incidence of highwaymen these days is truly scandalous, as everyone says. Perhaps the very letter is even now lying in some ditch with a dozen others, covered by a half-foot of mud, or some other, equally disagreeable substance." She pushed a plate of pastries to him. "Sweets, Uncle?"

He pushed the plate back. "None, thank you. Very well, perhaps your letter was waylaid. It cannot matter now, since I am here, and have found you. I needn't say that we have all been anxious at home for any news of you. Mr. Hyde, in fact, was fully prepared to accompany me here. I could scarcely convince him that . . . well, discretion required that I come by myself."

"Yes, it would have been an imposition on Lady Pym, to expect her to put up more than one extra person."

"Lady Pym need not have worried. I did not plan to stop over myself — at least, not longer than you will require to put your affairs in order and prepare yourself to accompany me home."

"I beg your pardon? You expect me to quit Pym House, with no more preamble than that? I am sorry you have so little regard for my hostess, Uncle, who has certainly been more than generous."

"I daresay you are the one with little enough regard for the woman, to have imposed on her resources, and her privacy, as long as you have! I shall not require any arguments from you, my girl. I have been more than lenient as it is. Mr. Hyde's feelings, too, ought to be considered. He has waited long and patiently for some response to his suit."

"Mr. Hyde has had as much response already as he may expect. I am sorry, Uncle, but I have considered the matter and that is my final decision." She rose, rather stiffly, he thought, and strolled to the windows. "We ought to have more light in here, don't you agree?" She parted the dense curtains with a swift tug on a tasseled cord. "There, that's much better."

Lionel rose too, his arms rigid at his sides. A month with a fine household had not altered Sarah's abrasive disposition at all, he noted with grave disappointment. How long would it take him to strip away this new, even haughtier varnish? How misguidedly indulgent he had been even to allow this holiday in the first place! "I think you are behaving with great insolence, Sarah. I do not think we need debate Mr. Hyde's merits yet again. For heaven's sake, leave that curtain alone! Do you intend to pull it off the wall?"

Sarah released the cord and began to stare at the open doors. Lionel twisted his head around in irritation. When he saw nothing, he motioned for her to return to the couch.

"I think my hostess would agree with me that Mr. Hyde is not a suitable match for any intelligent woman," she ventured, refocusing her eyes on her uncle with an effort. Where was Augusta? Surely she needn't climb the curtains, as well, and swing the length of the windows a few times? "The . . . er, sort of people I have encountered here have made me realize that all the more."

"Your hostess is obviously a woman of good sense and breeding. She therefore would assent to no such thing. Those in her position — and mine — have far more insight in these matters, and you, my dear, would be well advised to take notice of that fact!"

"I cannot believe there is much that does escape Miss Lindsay's attention," an authoritative voice asserted from behind him. He turned as Augusta swept between them, dabbed with scent and richly attired.

Lionel was stunned, that much Sarah found obvious. Less obvious, she hoped, was her own dazzled smile, which spread across her face in spite of Augusta's earlier instructions to avoid any emotional extremes whatsoever in his presence. Dashing across the parlor to smother her in kisses would, she supposed, provide an unfortunate example of precisely what not to do.

Augusta offered Lionel not one, but both hands. "Please do forgive my tardiness," she chirped. "I felt sure you'd indulge me, but then my impression that we're all the oldest of friends is only a fancy of mine. I presume too far, I'm sure."

"No, not at all." Lionel did not smile, disapproving of the practice as a whole for gentlemen, but he had to admire the clean, wiry fingers he gripped. Lady Pym was no novice at hostessing, he could tell. Clearly, the tedious part of the interview was past.

They returned to their seats, Lady Pym squeezing Sarah's hand briefly before reaching for a sweet. She told Lionel quite frankly about the loneliness she had experienced after her husband's death, and her inability to locate a companion of her own class and intelligence. She thanked Lionel for allowing Sarah to remain on as her guest perhaps a little longer than propriety allowed. He was, she could see, a man of great shrewdness and sensitivity. Lionel was now more inclined to believe that a letter of explanation had been dispatched and waylaid. Lady Pym would have insisted, despite the protests Sarah without doubt had raised, that one be written.

Lionel also had to admit that the two made a very appealing, very feminine picture seated together and chatting so blithely. His older female acquaintances had always assured him that such attachments between young women were a necessary prerequisite for any more serious affection for a suitor. Sarah's sheltered girlhood had prevented her from developing a proper sense of the sentimental, he decided. Perhaps it had been unreasonable of him to expect her to accept Mr. Hyde without the benefit of some harmless schoolgirl embroilments.

"Well, Lady Pym, I can see that Sarah has been well-served by your attentions. I hope, too, that you will come to call on us whenever convenient. I will be happy to return your generosity in any way I am able."

"I thank you indeed." Augusta induced him to accept the last pastry. As he picked it up, he noticed

187

Sarah's eyes flick uncertainly across to her hostess. Augusta did not look at her. Had Sarah intended Lady Pym to remonstrate with him? How little the girl knew of mature, and prudent, demeanor. At any moment he expected to see her lower lip curl down in defiance. He sighed, tasting the pastry's sweet cream as it tickled his throat. Even a noblewoman's impeccable influence could accomplish only so much with Sarah. Augusta Pym felt the same way, apparently, for she was patting Sarah's rigid hands. Poor child, he could almost hear her saying.

"Perhaps you would like a tour of the grounds, Mr. Lindsay? It would be nice to stretch, especially for you after such a long ride."

"That would be very agreeable, Lady Pym." Lionel stood up, and offered a hand up to her. She accepted it with pleasure. Though he was not a titled man, Lionel smugly reflected that he, at least, had had no difficulty respecting and learning to emulate his betters.

They circled the house, Augusta supplying various anecdotes about the building of a particular wing or the installation of a favorite shrub. Lionel listened with the polite concentration expected of him, offering a comparison with his own home when prompted, and praising the orchard, which they stopped just short of entering. Some cottagers pruning the trees stopped to tip their brown caps at Augusta, who signaled back. Lionel was not surprised to observe her benevolence toward her staff. A woman of her secure position would not have to assert her authority through the humiliation of others. He only wished Sarah were as observant as he was, and could appreciate such subtleties for herself.

At the end of their walk, Lady Pym turned to him abruptly. "At this hour, your niece usually prefers to spend some time by herself. She has, I believe, a few letters to answer." Sarah stared at her blankly. This new twist they had not rehearsed. A bolt of fear burned through her when Augusta touched her uncle's sleeve. "Perhaps you would join me in my study. There are things we might discuss."

"Delighted," Lionel said.

The interview lasted for the better part of an hour. Sarah read in the salon for a while, found the constant sight of the locked bookcase too painful, and retreated to her room. There she found Valerie sorting through her clothing and arranging her dressing gown on a hook in the wardrobe.

"You've seen Uncle Lionel?" Sarah asked without preamble.

"Yes, Miss. We'll be leaving, then?"

"I don't know. Lady Pym is with him. Charming him. She's very good at that."

"He's not very angry with us, then?"

"Oh, he'd never show it in front of Lady Pym. We'll soon know, I daresay."

Valerie had paused with a green dress in her hands. Sarah saw that she was smoothing the same wrinkle over and over, with no apparent result.

"Valerie, I intend to stay at Pym House. I'm going to resist Uncle Lionel as best I can, as long as Augusta wants me to. I think you know why . . ."

"We talked about it, Miss, I remember." Valerie's manner grew more evasive. Sarah knew the question she had decided to ask was unnecessary. "I have been thinking, Miss, that I might go on to Bath after all. There's plenty of work there, all the girls here say, lots of old dowagers wanting a hand, people with nice houses trying to marry their daughters off. And the air is very good, I'm told . . . oh, Miss, I am sorry to leave you."

"That's all right, Valerie. I wish you the best. How long will you stay here?"

"Well, I was hoping maybe until the autumn. Bath isn't very comfortable in the heat, I'm sure, and I want a family that's fairly settled."

"I'll write you the letters, then, whenever you ask me. And I can inquire from Mrs. Waterbury. Perhaps she knows someone suitable."

Valerie hung the dress up at last. She stood before Sarah not moving, looking chastised. "I do thank you, Miss."

"We all do what we must. I shall walk outside, I think, if someone needs me." Sarah trotted down the staircase with a clouded feeling. Betsy was just carrying a tray of claret and two glasses into the study. Without bothering to find a cloak, Sarah strode onto the rear terrace. One of the workmen had moved out of the orchard and into the hedges. She watched him trimming back branches with a curved knife that flashed in the sunlight. A little girl with tangled hair and bare feet was watching him, too, from the other side of the shrubs. He called to her for a piece of string, and she obediently surrendered it.

Sarah walked over to the child, who eyed her with unabashed curiosity. "You're Miss Lindsay," she muttered, in a tone bordering on the accusatory.

"That's right."

"Don't be bothering the lady, Tessie," the hedge-cutter glanced up and admonished, then went back to tying his string.

"I've seen you and Lady Pym out riding," the girl continued. "She comes to call on us sometimes, at the cottage. We take her in the kitchen, and sometimes we can give her tea. Right around Christmas she always sends chickens."

"It's a goose, Tessie," the hedge-cutter corrected. "Usually a goose."

"Whatever. I say it's very like a chicken. Next year, you know, my sister's coming up to the house. Going to start helping Lothaire, Lady Pym says. Then she's going to have to learn some more ciphering. There's going to be a school or something, my mother says."

"Your mother is right. All the cottagers will learn to read, and work with numbers."

The girl's blunt nose wrinkled. "Not me. Mother says I'll have to go, too, when I'm older. But I shan't. I want to stay with the horses. If Lady Pym comes to the cottage to make me go, I'll hide behind the privy until she goes away again."

"Tessie! You show some respect for the lady!"

"It's all right." Sarah smiled as the girl thrust out her lower lip and raced off across the lawn. "A good many of the children will feel the same, I'm sure."

"Can't say I see the need of it myself, not really." The man stood upright, wiped his upper lip, and flexed his fingers. "Girls are needed round the house most days. Still, it's Lady Pym's green things I live off, isn't it? Can't argue."

191

Sarah murmured some reply and went back into the house. The pungent smell of his perspiration followed her. She was crossing the foyer again when Uncle Lionel stepped into her path.

"You have found a true friend in Lady Pym, Sarah. Did you know that?"

"Yes, Uncle, I did." The apprehension which had now seized her all over again drove the latent sarcasm from her voice.

Lionel, not noticing, locked his hands behind his starched coattails. "I am not sure you have fully learned to comprehend honor and gratitude yet, but I am still optimistic that time and guidance will enlighten you."

The study door clicked open again, and Augusta stood watching them. Her lips curved in almost smug satisfaction. Sarah's heart began to beat harshly.

"I take it that a continued association with Lady Pym is acceptable to you?"

"It is, Uncle."

"Then I trust that your conduct within these walls will always remain a source of pride to me. Lady Pym knows that my own home stands ready to receive you again at any time."

"I don't think I'll be forced to put her out." Augusta laughed, crossing her arms and leaning in the threshold.

Lionel stayed to dinner that evening, then set off to pay another call. After that, he would continue on to Bath. Augusta tactfully made no plans to meet him again there.

After his departure, the two stood in the drive and watched the dusk settle around them. The twitter of insects and nestlings grew higher in pitch. Augusta's eyes glittered like still gray puddles of seawater as Sarah basked in them, her arm stealing around her hostess's waist.

"Solicitors are coming day after tomorrow," Augusta reminded her softly. "Don't forget you're to meet them, to discuss our cottagers."

"Our," Sarah repeated the word, savoring it. "Are you going to tell me how you convinced Uncle Lionel?"

"I do not consider myself an old-fashioned woman, but on occasion I can impersonate one. Your uncle enjoyed that."

"You didn't tell him the truth . . . !"

Augusta's clear laugh interrupted the crickets. "Heavens, I'm not sure they ever did that in the old days either! No, love, that would never have served us."

"Then tell me. I deserve to know."

"Yes." Her laughter faded. "You do."

"Well?"

"Well, in the first place I forwarded some capital to your uncle, so that he may add my name to one of his new ventures in Scotland. Then . . ." Augusta pulled free, disconcerting Sarah, and strode a few paces along the gravel alone.

"Then?"

"Then your uncle and I drew up what is called, perhaps appropriately, a gentlemen's agreement, and each put our names to it. It is an agreement concerning you, Sarah. Specifically, that I will accept a percentage of financial responsibility for you, and complete responsibility for . . . for finding you a match. At that time I will augment your dowry substantially, seeing that I will have no daughters of my own." Even before Sarah's jaw had fully dropped, she hurried on. "it was the best way, surely you can see that. And I didn't lose my head — I made certain he could impose no time limit. We could take fifteen years to find someone suitable, even longer. By that time, he'll have no hold over you."

"You've bought me?"

"No, love, no. I'm giving your freedom back to you."

"It wasn't a new guardian I wanted."

"And it isn't one you've gained. Sarah, listen. We are equals, we are. But these games do have rules. The better we play, the freer we are. Do you see that? Of course I would alter things if I could. If you can, then do! Only tell me first, and I'll help you."

Sarah couldn't answer. She hugged her arms tighter, and waited for the gloom to envelop the ground they stood on. Augusta waited, too.

"It was a game my mother didn't want to play either." Sarah poked at a stone with her toe.

Augusta nodded. "If she had known how, perhaps she'd be ranging the world even now."

"I wouldn't be here, in that case."

"Please, Sarah, don't make me contemplate such a possibility, not even for the sake of an argument."

Sarah shrugged off a sudden chill. Augusta's arms were there, enfolding her again. Yes, she was both bound and free. Free of Lionel, and of Isabel. Surely those advantages outweighed the discomfort of being locked by name to some obscure sheet of foolscap tucked under Augusta's blotter? Augusta needed no such document to claim her.

"Is remaining here really not what you want?" Augusta's warm whisper caressed her ear. "Did you lie to poor Uncle Lionel, too?"

"No." The little smile of pleasure crept up on her, and before she could stifle it Augusta was wearing it, too. "I do want to stay, very much, those fifteen years you spoke of and more. There really aren't many marriageable peers left in England these days, are there?"

"Almost none." Augusta rocked Sarah off her feet for a moment. "None good enough for you, especially."

The sweet taste of their lips merging left Sarah aching for more. They were safe enough here from any curious eyes, bathed as they were in the shadows of twilight. Nevertheless, it began to seem to Sarah that they were actually in the center of a great pool of light, spreading around them in a brilliant hot undulation.

CHAPTER 13

Waterloo Day, the eighteenth of June, descended damp and cool. The newssheets, usually full of patriotic diatribe and puffery, today confined themselves to somber reports of the King's worsening health. William had taken a downward turn just a few days before, and now seemed bedridden for the last time. National anxiety ran high for the next seventy-two hours. Princess Drina, wisely, vanished from public view, withdrawing with her mother to the privacy of Kensington Palace.

On the morning of the twenty-first, Lucy Gwinn

arrived in the company of Margaret, who had summarily dispensed with the illness in the Gwinn household and had stayed on a few weeks longer as their guest. Although the skies were still threatening, Augusta entertained Miss Gwinn at the little stone table at the corner of the garden. Gossip around Bath was likewise concerned with the King's imminent demise and what lay in store for the country once Alexandrina Victoria had replaced him.

"What they fear most is the German influence," Lucy said, peering down her spectacles at Sarah, their tea growing cold in front of them. "They all feel she'll marry one, of course, and they say she speaks English like a true Hanoverian."

"We'll go to London to see her." Augusta nodded, lately engrossed in such speculation. "Not now, when there'll scarcely be room for a horse to stand, but when everything calms down again."

"They won't have the coronation straight away. She'll have to go into mourning. During the interval she'll probably be rather visible."

"True. What I'd like most is an audience with her. I suppose that will be nearly impossible now."

"You and I, in our sovereign's presence?" Sarah had to laugh. "What frightens me most about Augusta is that she always manages to bring her fancies about somehow. One day she'll simply drag me off to London, never stopping to notice that I'm wearing a gown with a button lost, and have ink smudges on my face."

"Our Queen would be taken with you anyway. What woman of wit and exuberance would not?"

Lucy watched the two tease each other, then stirred her tea and sought her own reflection in her spoon. "I must confess," she ventured, "that I am a bit surprised to find you still here, Miss Lindsay . . . much less planning to open a schoolroom, of all things. That is a demanding task by anyone's standards."

"We shall expect whatever assistance and advice you and Dorothy can provide, of course," Augusta said. "We have not the benefit of your experience."

"Some of my experience you would not consider beneficial." Lucy's tone soured unexpectedly. "Perhaps if more people sought in themselves the strength you seem to have found, Miss Lindsay, we would not be forced to look upon the sort of despair and poverty I have encountered in my travels. I used to think it well and good to fortify my spirit with the love of language and the tonic of the printed page. Only recently have I come to see what an utter fool I have been." Lucy's lips tightened, and for a moment she looked older than her true years. "You have seen the illustrations in the periodicals, no doubt. I have seen the realities."

"Yes, we've seen them," Augusta replied softly.

Sarah mulled over these words, too. No doubt Miss Gwinn was exposed, every day, to sufferings and outrages that would never penetrate the trimmed hedgerows of Pym House. Were she and Augusta absolving themselves of guilt concerning the supposed sins of the flesh, only to slip unwittingly into the far more disgusting mire of overall heartlessness? For too long now, they had given almost no thought at all to anything but their own pleasures, or at best the partial education of a handful of country children, while thousands wasted away, cold and ignorant, in cities only a few hours distant. The illustrations Lucy spoke of had indeed made her cringe, made her full stomach twist. Yet what had she done, besides turn the page and ring for fresh coffee, or seek oblivion in Augusta's indulgent embrace?

"The world mutates a little every day," Augusta said finally, pushing her sugared tea to one side and lacing her hands together. "Within a few hours, we shall be a new England. Ultimately, it will not be our Queen who makes the most difference, but the acts we are moved to accomplish in her name. As for me, my blood has never lain stagnant."

At the sound of a rider, Sarah allowed herself to look past the shrubs to the pathway. "Well," she said, gesturing in surprise, "it's Angela Lamb."

They all turned. Angela was riding hard, and straight toward them. Her face was high in color, and a cluster of damp iron-gray curls lay flat against her forehead, her tall hat knocked askew by sustained motion. When she reached the perimeter of the garden, she slid to her feet and closed the remaining distance with a frenzied dash through the lilacs.

"Well, it's over," she panted. "King William is gone."

Augusta leaped up at once. "No! Are you certain?"

Angela nodded rapidly. "Yes, yes, my nephew is in London. He sent a rider straight to me as soon as he'd heard it confirmed. He went at about two in the morning. Not difficult, Winchell said, with one of those funny religious turns at the end. Fancy King

William calling out to the Church, with his last breath! But I imagine when the hand of God is at your throat, and squeezing . . ."

"Drina's been proclaimed, then?"

"Yes, yes, that's all over with now. And she's not to be called Drina any longer. She's Victoria, our Queen."

The four of them digested this. Augusta's hand found Sarah's, and likewise Lucy and Angela reached out to them, too. They stood linked together, as if they all were preparing to launch into some ridiculous May Dance, while the swollen clouds rolled overhead. Only once did a sliver of white light jab through, and glint off Angela's temple.

"Long live the Queen," said Augusta.

EPILOGUE

April, 1838:

The country's year of mourning for King William IV had ended. The coronation festivities, including a rash of balls, feasts, and concerts, would begin in May. Augusta had taken a townhouse for the occasion, and within a week of arriving had secured promising introductions for herself and Sarah. The path to the Queen's doorstep was growing shorter.

They received a good many callers during their first week in the city, old friends of Augusta's and a few of Sir Lewis's. Two of Uncle Lionel's business partners sent gifts, though Augusta procrastinated in inviting them to tea. Instead, she and Sarah used their afternoons for sightseeing. Augusta caused a minor stir when she challenged some onlookers to a race up St. Paul's Cathedral steps. Worse, they accepted. She won easily.

The morning after they had attended a particularly entertaining ball, Augusta took her tea alone in her downstairs sitting room. She had left Sarah sleeping upstairs, sweetly disheveled with a few rose-petals caught in her hair. Augusta found three in her own hairbrush as well.

Betsy brought her a plate of warm bread and jam. Next to the jam-pot lay an envelope. She picked it up, questioning with her eyes.

"Left this morning, mum, by one of those messenger fellows. Running 'im ragged, he said, with all these parties and all."

"Rather early in the day for an invitation," Augusta said.

Betsy shrugged. "Maybe 'e forgot it last night."

"One way to find out." Augusta read it with some surprise. Lillian Hamilton had signed it. The date was indeed that of the evening before. The message was short and significant. "Dear Gussie," she read, "It's taken some time, but I've found what you wanted. You might have known you could rely on me. I stumbled a bit due to the fact that the subject I sought relocated to France circa 1828. She did not survive the next winter, I fear. Still, I have made contact with someone who can help you. She'll come to call on Tuesday — that's tomorrow — at eleven o'clock. So sorry for the short notice, but she's on a tight schedule herself. I only just caught her. I won't be more specific than that, since I know you enjoy a puzzle. Yours, best, etc."

One phrase stood out in Augusta's mind. Today at eleven. Hastily she checked her watch. Nearly ten now.

"Gracious!" she said, and dashed upstairs. She sat beside Sarah and shook her. Sarah rolled over, floundered, and stared at her in surprise. "Love, I'm sorry. But you have to get up. We're going to have a caller."

"Do you need me for that?"

"This time I do. You see, she's actually coming to see you."

Miss Antonia Marche came at precisely eleven. Mrs. Hamilton had briefed her well; she walked directly to Sarah, put out her gloved hand, and announced herself as Mrs. Catherine Hudson Marche's daughter.

"Our mothers were the closest of friends," she informed the stunned Sarah. "Although my mother is dead, she spoke of yours often. She was the light of her life, she said always. My sister was even named for her. I never met her, of course, but through my mother's stories and letters I have come to know her well. When Mrs. Hamilton explained your loss, I felt I should call. Everyone deserves to know her mother, especially if she was as loved as Emilia Lindsay."

"Mrs. . . . Mrs. Hamilton?" Sarah choked. She barely knew the woman, except for meeting her briefly at Augusta's Christmas gathering.

At this point, Augusta smoothly cut in. "We are so pleased to meet you, Miss Marche. Betsy, will you show Miss Marche into the sitting room and bring tea? I believe, Miss Marche, this is a matter better discussed between Sarah and yourself in private. Therefore, I will withdraw until you have talked."

"Very well." Miss Marche started after Betsy, then paused. "I have some of their letters, Miss Lindsay, and I have brought them. I think you might benefit from our going through them together."

"Yes, yes, I'm sure that would be lovely." When she was alone with Augusta, Sarah turned to her. For a long time, she said nothing.

"I did not arrange this," said Augusta. "I wrote to Lillian Hamilton a year ago. I was certain there was more to your mother than what Lionel told you. I wanted you to know, if there was. Are . . . are you angry?"

"I had thought that part of my life was long over."

"Your mother will always be with you, as long as you're alive. Don't you think she deserves vindication?"

"Vindication, yes, if it were justified. In the present case, I think the details that might be uncovered would prove considerably . . . embarrassing."

"Embarrassing because the circumstances of your birth cannot be altered?" Augusta had crossed her arms.

"In part . . ."

"Entirely."

"Augusta, how can you hope to understand? Your

204

lineage will never be questioned — your blood is as purely gentry as it could possibly be. But what of me? I have no claim even to the surname I have been using all my life!"

"You regret being born, then."

Sarah furrowed her brow into a warm frown. She was behaving abominably to Augusta, of that she was well aware. "No," she whispered, hoping to make her contrition obvious, although she was not in her own judgment quite successful. "Not now, dearest. For that I have you to extend my gratitude — and I do. What could be gained, however, by dragging out a poor disgraced woman's name yet again as an unfortunate example of a soul corrupted by worldly experience? I must respect her memory to that extent, don't you see?"

"Oh, really, Sarah." To Sarah's relief, Augusta seemed neither angry nor insulted by her protests, merely impatient. She waved one hand in front of her as if to dismiss Sarah's misgivings like so much stale air. "Does Miss Marche look as though she's here to slander anyone? What she is eager to tell you, I think, is that your mother was not in fact the ogre your dear Uncle Lionel has so long made her out to be. His own shame, however misplaced, is something he will have to learn to accept for himself. You hold out my exceedingly patrician lineage as a perfect example of gentility? Well, then, the most benign use I could possibly make of it would be to extend the forgiveness my class seldom does in matters involving human nature. So your mother walked a little apart from the well-trod path prepared for ladies of her status. Haven't we done the same?" She moved closer to Sarah and brushed her fingers against her arm. "Do you consider ourselves wicked, too?"

"Of course not, love." Sarah's eyes were moistening. She had to clear her throat. Her palm fluttered up to Augusta's cheek, though she could not meet her eyes right away.

"It will be hard to acknowledge that Uncle Lionel's wisdom may yet again have misled you," Augusta assured her gently. "But I think she deserves to be remembered as the kind of woman who could inspire the sort of devotion Miss Marche's mother apparently held for her, don't you? Rather the kind of woman you are in my eyes, in fact."

"Dearest," Sarah whispered, the last vestiges of her frustration melting as she pressed her face against Augusta's.

"I hate to leave you, even for a moment," Sarah said at last, smiling. "But I'd better go and hear Miss Marche out, don't you agree? She has traveled such a long way." But they stood for several more minutes, enfolded in that more pleasant brand of warmth, saying nothing but feeling eternity shelter their union.

A few of the publications of
THE NAIAD PRESS, INC.
P.O. Box 10543 • Tallahassee, Florida 32302
Phone (904) 539-5965
Mail orders welcome. Please include 15% postage.

THAT OLD STUDEBAKER by Lee Lynch. 272 pp. Andy's affair
with Regina and her attachment to her beloved car.
ISBN 0-941483-82-7 $9.95

PASSION'S LEGACY by Lori Paige. 224 pp. Sarah is swept into
the arms of Augusta Pym in this delightful historical romance.
ISBN 0-941483-81-9   8.95

THE PROVIDENCE FILE by Amanda Kyle Williams. 256 pp.
Second espionage thriller featuring lesbian agent Madison McGuire
ISBN 0-941483-92-4   8.95

I LEFT MY HEART by Jaye Maiman. 320 pp. A Robin Miller
Mystery. First in a series.   ISBN 0-941483-72-X   9.95

THE PRICE OF SALT by Patricia Highsmith (writing as Claire
Morgan). 288 pp. Classic lesbian novel, first issued in 1952 . . .
acknowledged by its author under her own, very famous, name.
ISBN 1-56280-003-5   8.95

SIDE BY SIDE by Isabel Miller. 256 pp. From beloved author of
Patience and Sarah.   ISBN 0-941483-77-0   8.95

SOUTHBOUND by Sheila Ortiz Taylor. 240 pp. Hilarious sequel
to Faultline.   ISBN 0-941483-78-9   8.95

STAYING POWER: LONG TERM LESBIAN COUPLES
by Susan E. Johnson. 352 pp. Joys of coupledom.
ISBN 0-941-483-75-4   12.95

SLICK by Camarin Grae. 304 pp. Exotic, erotic adventure.
ISBN 0-941483-74-6   9.95

NINTH LIFE by Lauren Wright Douglas. 256 pp. A Caitlin
Reece mystery. 2nd in a series.   ISBN 0-941483-50-9   8.95

PLAYERS by Robbi Sommers. 192 pp. Sizzling, erotic novel.
ISBN 0-941483-73-8   8.95

MURDER AT RED ROOK RANCH by Dorothy Tell. 224 pp.
First Poppy Dillworth adventure.   ISBN 0-941483-80-0   8.95

LESBIAN SURVIVAL MANUAL by Rhonda Dicksion.
112 pp. Cartoons!   ISBN 0-941483-71-1   8.95

A ROOM FULL OF WOMEN by Elisabeth Nonas. 256 pp.
Contemporary Lesbian lives.   ISBN 0-941483-69-X   8.95

MURDER IS RELATIVE by Karen Saum. 256 pp. The first
Brigid Donovan mystery. ISBN 0-941483-70-3   8.95

PRIORITIES by Lynda Lyons 288 pp. Science fiction with
a twist. ISBN 0-941483-66-5   8.95

THEME FOR DIVERSE INSTRUMENTS by Jane Rule. 208
pp. Powerful romantic lesbian stories. ISBN 0-941483-63-0   8.95

LESBIAN QUERIES by Hertz & Ertman. 112 pp. The questions
you were too embarrassed to ask. ISBN 0-941483-67-3   8.95

CLUB 12 by Amanda Kyle Williams. 288 pp. Espionage thriller
featuring a lesbian agent! ISBN 0-941483-64-9   8.95

DEATH DOWN UNDER by Claire McNab. 240 pp. 3rd Det.
Insp. Carol Ashton mystery. ISBN 0-941483-39-8   8.95

MONTANA FEATHERS by Penny Hayes. 256 pp. Vivian and
Elizabeth find love in frontier Montana. ISBN 0-941483-61-4   8.95

CHESAPEAKE PROJECT by Phyllis Horn. 304 pp. Jessie &
Meredith in perilous adventure. ISBN 0-941483-58-4   8.95

LIFESTYLES by Jackie Calhoun. 224 pp. Contemporary Lesbian
lives and loves. ISBN 0-941483-57-6   8.95

VIRAGO by Karen Marie Christa Minns. 208 pp. Darsen has
chosen Ginny. ISBN 0-941483-56-8   8.95

WILDERNESS TREK by Dorothy Tell. 192 pp. Six women on
vacation learning "new" skills. ISBN 0-941483-60-6   8.95

MURDER BY THE BOOK by Pat Welch. 256 pp. A Helen
Black Mystery. First in a series. ISBN 0-941483-59-2   8.95

BERRIGAN by Vicki P. McConnell. 176 pp. Youthful Lesbian-
romantic, idealistic Berrigan. ISBN 0-941483-55-X   8.95

LESBIANS IN GERMANY by Lillian Faderman & B. Eriksson.
128 pp. Fiction, poetry, essays. ISBN 0-941483-62-2   8.95

THE BEVERLY MALIBU by Katherine V. Forrest. 288 pp. A
Kate Delafield Mystery. 3rd in a series. ISBN 0-941483-47-9   16.95

THERE'S SOMETHING I'VE BEEN MEANING TO TELL
YOU Ed. by Loralee MacPike. 288 pp. Gay men and lesbians
coming out to their children. ISBN 0-941483-44-4   9.95
ISBN 0-941483-54-1   16.95

LIFTING BELLY by Gertrude Stein. Ed. by Rebecca Mark. 104
pp. Erotic poetry. ISBN 0-941483-51-7   8.95
ISBN 0-941483-53-3   14.95

ROSE PENSKI by Roz Perry. 192 pp. Adult lovers in a long-term
relationship. ISBN 0-941483-37-1   8.95

AFTER THE FIRE by Jane Rule. 256 pp. Warm, human novel
by this incomparable author. ISBN 0-941483-45-2   8.95

SUE SLATE, PRIVATE EYE by Lee Lynch. 176 pp. The gay
folk of Peacock Alley are *all* cats.   ISBN 0-941483-52-5   8.95

CHRIS by Randy Salem. 224 pp. Golden oldie. Handsome Chris
and her adventures.   ISBN 0-941483-42-8   8.95

THREE WOMEN by March Hastings. 232 pp. Golden oldie. A
triangle among wealthy sophisticates.   ISBN 0-941483-43-6   8.95

RICE AND BEANS by Valeria Taylor. 232 pp. Love and
romance on poverty row.   ISBN 0-941483-41-X   8.95

PLEASURES by Robbi Sommers. 204 pp. Unprecedented
eroticism.   ISBN 0-941483-49-5   8.95

EDGEWISE by Camarin Grae. 372 pp. Spellbinding
adventure.   ISBN 0-941483-19-3   9.95

FATAL REUNION by Claire McNab. 216 pp. 2nd Det. Inspec.
Carol Ashton mystery.   ISBN 0-941483-40-1   8.95

KEEP TO ME STRANGER by Sarah Aldridge. 372 pp. Romance
set in a department store dynasty.   ISBN 0-941483-38-X   9.95

HEARTSCAPE by Sue Gambill. 204 pp. American lesbian in
Portugal.   ISBN 0-941483-33-9   8.95

IN THE BLOOD by Lauren Wright Douglas. 252 pp. Lesbian
science fiction adventure fantasy   ISBN 0-941483-22-3   8.95

THE BEE'S KISS by Shirley Verel. 216 pp. Delicate, delicious
romance.   ISBN 0-941483-36-3   8.95

RAGING MOTHER MOUNTAIN by Pat Emmerson. 264 pp.
Furosa Firechild's adventures in Wonderland.   ISBN 0-941483-35-5   8.95

IN EVERY PORT by Karin Kallmaker. 228 pp. Jessica's sexy,
adventuresome travels.   ISBN 0-941483-37-7   8.95

OF LOVE AND GLORY by Evelyn Kennedy. 192 pp. Exciting
WWII romance.   ISBN 0-941483-32-0   8.95

CLICKING STONES by Nancy Tyler Glenn. 288 pp. Love
transcending time.   ISBN 0-941483-31-2   8.95

SURVIVING SISTERS by Gail Pass. 252 pp. Powerful love
story.   ISBN 0-941483-16-9   8.95

SOUTH OF THE LINE by Catherine Ennis. 216 pp. Civil War
adventure.   ISBN 0-941483-29-0   8.95

WOMAN PLUS WOMAN by Dolores Klaich. 300 pp. Supurb
Lesbian overview.   ISBN 0-941483-28-2   9.95

SLOW DANCING AT MISS POLLY'S by Sheila Ortiz Taylor.
96 pp. Lesbian Poetry   ISBN 0-941483-30-4   7.95

DOUBLE DAUGHTER by Vicki P. McConnell. 216 pp. A Nyla
Wade Mystery, third in the series.   ISBN 0-941483-26-6   8.95

HEAVY GILT by Delores Klaich. 192 pp. Lesbian detective/
disappearing homophobes/upper class gay society.
ISBN 0-941483-25-8   8.95

THE FINER GRAIN by Denise Ohio. 216 pp. Brilliant young
college lesbian novel.   ISBN 0-941483-11-8   8.95

THE AMAZON TRAIL by Lee Lynch. 216 pp. Life, travel & lore
of famous lesbian author.   ISBN 0-941483-27-4   8.95

HIGH CONTRAST by Jessie Lattimore. 264 pp. Women of the
Crystal Palace.   ISBN 0-941483-17-7   8.95

OCTOBER OBSESSION by Meredith More. Josie's rich, secret
Lesbian life.   ISBN 0-941483-18-5   8.95

LESBIAN CROSSROADS by Ruth Baetz. 276 pp. Contemporary
Lesbian lives.   ISBN 0-941483-21-5   9.95

BEFORE STONEWALL: THE MAKING OF A GAY AND
LESBIAN COMMUNITY by Andrea Weiss & Greta Schiller.
96 pp., 25 illus.   ISBN 0-941483-20-7   7.95

WE WALK THE BACK OF THE TIGER by Patricia A. Murphy.
192 pp. Romantic Lesbian novel/beginning women's movement.
ISBN 0-941483-13-4   8.95

SUNDAY'S CHILD by Joyce Bright. 216 pp. Lesbian athletics, at
last the novel about sports.   ISBN 0-941483-12-6   8.95

OSTEN'S BAY by Zenobia N. Vole. 204 pp. Sizzling adventure
romance set on Bonaire.   ISBN 0-941483-15-0   8.95

LESSONS IN MURDER by Claire McNab. 216 pp. 1st Det. Inspec.
Carol Ashton mystery — erotic tension!.   ISBN 0-941483-14-2   8.95

YELLOWTHROAT by Penny Hayes. 240 pp. Margarita, bandit,
kidnaps Julia.   ISBN 0-941483-10-X   8.95

SAPPHISTRY: THE BOOK OF LESBIAN SEXUALITY by
Pat Califia. 3d edition, revised. 208 pp.   ISBN 0-941483-24-X   8.95

CHERISHED LOVE by Evelyn Kennedy. 192 pp. Erotic
Lesbian love story.   ISBN 0-941483-08-8   8.95

LAST SEPTEMBER by Helen R. Hull. 208 pp. Six stories & a
glorious novella.   ISBN 0-941483-09-6   8.95

THE SECRET IN THE BIRD by Camarin Grae. 312 pp. Striking,
psychological suspense novel.   ISBN 0-941483-05-3   8.95

TO THE LIGHTNING by Catherine Ennis. 208 pp. Romantic
Lesbian 'Robinson Crusoe' adventure.   ISBN 0-941483-06-1   8.95

THE OTHER SIDE OF VENUS by Shirley Verel. 224 pp.
Luminous, romantic love story.   ISBN 0-941483-07-X   8.95

DREAMS AND SWORDS by Katherine V. Forrest. 192 pp.
Romantic, erotic, imaginative stories.   ISBN 0-941483-03-7   8.95

MEMORY BOARD by Jane Rule. 336 pp. Memorable novel
about an aging Lesbian couple.   ISBN 0-941483-02-9   9.95

THE ALWAYS ANONYMOUS BEAST by Lauren Wright
Douglas. 224 pp. A Caitlin Reece mystery. First in a series.
                                        ISBN 0-941483-04-5   8.95

SEARCHING FOR SPRING by Patricia A. Murphy. 224 pp.
Novel about the recovery of love.   ISBN 0-941483-00-2   8.95

DUSTY'S QUEEN OF HEARTS DINER by Lee Lynch. 240 pp.
Romantic blue-collar novel.   ISBN 0-941483-01-0   8.95

PARENTS MATTER by Ann Muller. 240 pp. Parents'
relationships with Lesbian daughters and gay sons.
                                        ISBN 0-930044-91-6   9.95

THE PEARLS by Shelley Smith. 176 pp. Passion and fun in
the Caribbean sun.   ISBN 0-930044-93-2   7.95

MAGDALENA by Sarah Aldridge. 352 pp. Epic Lesbian novel
set on three continents.   ISBN 0-930044-99-1   8.95

THE BLACK AND WHITE OF IT by Ann Allen Shockley.
144 pp. Short stories.   ISBN 0-930044-96-7   7.95

SAY JESUS AND COME TO ME by Ann Allen Shockley. 288
pp. Contemporary romance.   ISBN 0-930044-98-3   8.95

LOVING HER by Ann Allen Shockley. 192 pp. Romantic love
story.   ISBN 0-930044-97-5   7.95

MURDER AT THE NIGHTWOOD BAR by Katherine V.
Forrest. 240 pp. A Kate Delafield mystery. Second in a series.
                                        ISBN 0-930044-92-4   8.95

ZOE'S BOOK by Gail Pass. 224 pp. Passionate, obsessive love
story.   ISBN 0-930044-95-9   7.95

WINGED DANCER by Camarin Grae. 228 pp. Erotic Lesbian
adventure story.   ISBN 0-930044-88-6   9.95

PAZ by Camarin Grae. 336 pp. Romantic Lesbian adventurer
with the power to change the world.   ISBN 0-930044-89-4   8.95

SOUL SNATCHER by Camarin Grae. 224 pp. A puzzle, an
adventure, a mystery -- Lesbian romance.   ISBN 0-930044-90-8   8.95

THE LOVE OF GOOD WOMEN by Isabel Miller. 224 pp.
Long-awaited new novel by the author of the beloved *Patience
and Sarah*.   ISBN 0-930044-81-9   8.95

THE HOUSE AT PELHAM FALLS by Brenda Weathers. 240
pp. Suspenseful Lesbian ghost story.   ISBN 0-930044-79-7   7.95

HOME IN YOUR HANDS by Lee Lynch. 240 pp. More stories
from the author of *Old Dyke Tales*.   ISBN 0-930044-80-0   7.95

EACH HAND A MAP by Anita Skeen. 112 pp. Real-life poems
that touch us all.   ISBN 0-930044-82-7   6.95

SURPLUS by Sylvia Stevenson. 342 pp. A classic early Lesbian
novel.   ISBN 0-930044-78-9   7.95

PEMBROKE PARK by Michelle Martin. 256 pp. Derring-do
and daring romance in Regency England.   ISBN 0-930044-77-0   7.95

THE LONG TRAIL by Penny Hayes. 248 pp. Vivid adventures
of two women in love in the old west.   ISBN 0-930044-76-2   8.95

HORIZON OF THE HEART by Shelley Smith. 192 pp. Hot
romance in summertime New England.   ISBN 0-930044-75-4   7.95

AN EMERGENCE OF GREEN by Katherine V. Forrest. 288
pp. Powerful novel of sexual discovery.   ISBN 0-930044-69-X   8.95

THE LESBIAN PERIODICALS INDEX edited by Claire
Potter. 432 pp. Author & subject index.   ISBN 0-930044-74-6   29.95

DESERT OF THE HEART by Jane Rule. 224 pp. A classic;
basis for the movie *Desert Hearts.*   ISBN 0-930044-73-8   8.95

SPRING FORWARD/FALL BACK by Sheila Ortiz Taylor.
288 pp. Literary novel of timeless love. ISBN 0-930044-70-3   7.95

FOR KEEPS by Elisabeth Nonas. 144 pp. Contemporary novel
about losing and finding love.   ISBN 0-930044-71-1   7.95

TORCHLIGHT TO VALHALLA by Gale Wilhelm. 128 pp.
Classic novel by a great Lesbian writer. ISBN 0-930044-68-1   7.95

LESBIAN NUNS: BREAKING SILENCE edited by Rosemary
Curb and Nancy Manahan. 432 pp. Unprecedented autobiographies
of religious life.   ISBN 0-930044-62-2   9.95

THE SWASHBUCKLER by Lee Lynch. 288 pp. Colorful novel
set in Greenwich Village in the sixties. ISBN 0-930044-66-5   8.95

MISFORTUNE'S FRIEND by Sarah Aldridge. 320 pp. Historical Lesbian novel set on two continents. ISBN 0-930044-67-3   7.95

A STUDIO OF ONE'S OWN by Ann Stokes. Edited by
Dolores Klaich. 128 pp. Autobiography.   ISBN 0-930044-64-9   7.95

SEX VARIANT WOMEN IN LITERATURE by Jeannette
Howard Foster. 448 pp. Literary history. ISBN 0-930044-65-7   8.95

A HOT-EYED MODERATE by Jane Rule. 252 pp. Hard-hitting
essays on gay life; writing; art.   ISBN 0-930044-57-6   7.95

INLAND PASSAGE AND OTHER STORIES by Jane Rule.
288 pp. Wide-ranging new collection.   ISBN 0-930044-56-8   7.95

WE TOO ARE DRIFTING by Gale Wilhelm. 128 pp. Timeless
Lesbian novel, a masterpiece.   ISBN 0-930044-61-4   6.95

AMATEUR CITY by Katherine V. Forrest. 224 pp. A Kate
Delafield mystery. First in a series.   ISBN 0-930044-55-X   8.95

THE SOPHIE HOROWITZ STORY by Sarah Schulman. 176
pp. Engaging novel of madcap intrigue.   ISBN 0-930044-54-1   7.95

THE BURNTON WIDOWS by Vickie P. McConnell. 272 pp. A
Nyla Wade mystery, second in the series. ISBN 0-930044-52-5   7.95

OLD DYKE TALES by Lee Lynch. 224 pp. Extraordinary
stories of our diverse Lesbian lives. ISBN 0-930044-51-7   8.95

DAUGHTERS OF A CORAL DAWN by Katherine V. Forrest.
240 pp. Novel set in a Lesbian new world. ISBN 0-930044-50-9   8.95

AGAINST THE SEASON by Jane Rule. 224 pp. Luminous,
complex novel of interrelationships. ISBN 0-930044-48-7   8.95

LOVERS IN THE PRESENT AFTERNOON by Kathleen
Fleming. 288 pp. A novel about recovery and growth.
ISBN 0-930044-46-0   8.95

TOOTHPICK HOUSE by Lee Lynch. 264 pp. Love between
two Lesbians of different classes. ISBN 0-930044-45-2   7.95

MADAME AURORA by Sarah Aldridge. 256 pp. Historical
novel featuring a charismatic "seer." ISBN 0-930044-44-4   7.95

CURIOUS WINE by Katherine V. Forrest. 176 pp. Passionate
Lesbian love story, a best-seller. ISBN 0-930044-43-6   8.95

BLACK LESBIAN IN WHITE AMERICA by Anita Cornwell.
141 pp. Stories, essays, autobiography. ISBN 0-930044-41-X   7.95

CONTRACT WITH THE WORLD by Jane Rule. 340 pp.
Powerful, panoramic novel of gay life. ISBN 0-930044-28-2   9.95

MRS. PORTER'S LETTER by Vicki P. McConnell. 224 pp.
The first Nyla Wade mystery. ISBN 0-930044-29-0   7.95

TO THE CLEVELAND STATION by Carol Anne Douglas.
192 pp. Interracial Lesbian love story. ISBN 0-930044-27-4   6.95

THE NESTING PLACE by Sarah Aldridge. 224 pp. A
three-woman triangle--love conquers all! ISBN 0-930044-26-6   7.95

THIS IS NOT FOR YOU by Jane Rule. 284 pp. A letter to a
beloved is also an intricate novel. ISBN 0-930044-25-8   8.95

FAULTLINE by Sheila Ortiz Taylor. 140 pp. Warm, funny,
literate story of a startling family. ISBN 0-930044-24-X   6.95

THE LESBIAN IN LITERATURE by Barbara Grier. 3d ed.
Foreword by Maida Tilchen. 240 pp. Comprehensive bibliography.
Literary ratings; rare photos. ISBN 0-930044-23-1   7.95

ANNA'S COUNTRY by Elizabeth Lang. 208 pp. A woman
finds her Lesbian identity. ISBN 0-930044-19-3   8.95

PRISM by Valerie Taylor. 158 pp. A love affair between two
women in their sixties. ISBN 0-930044-18-5   6.95

BLACK LESBIANS: AN ANNOTATED BIBLIOGRAPHY
compiled by J. R. Roberts. Foreword by Barbara Smith. 112 pp.
Award-winning bibliography. ISBN 0-930044-21-5   5.95

THE MARQUISE AND THE NOVICE by Victoria Ramstetter.
108 pp. A Lesbian Gothic novel.   ISBN 0-930044-16-9   6.95

OUTLANDER by Jane Rule. 207 pp. Short stories and essays
by one of our finest writers.   ISBN 0-930044-17-7   8.95

ALL TRUE LOVERS by Sarah Aldridge. 292 pp. Romantic
novel set in the 1930s and 1940s.   ISBN 0-930044-10-X   8.95

A WOMAN APPEARED TO ME by Renee Vivien. 65 pp. A
classic; translated by Jeannette H. Foster.   ISBN 0-930044-06-1   5.00

CYTHEREA'S BREATH by Sarah Aldridge. 240 pp. Romantic
novel about women's entrance into medicine.
                                         ISBN 0-930044-02-9   6.95

TOTTIE by Sarah Aldridge. 181 pp. Lesbian romance in the
turmoil of the sixties.   ISBN 0-930044-01-0   6.95

THE LATECOMER by Sarah Aldridge. 107 pp. A delicate love
story.   ISBN 0-930044-00-2   6.95

ODD GIRL OUT by Ann Bannon.   ISBN 0-930044-83-5   5.95

I AM A WOMAN by Ann Bannon.   ISBN 0-930044-84-3   5.95

WOMEN IN THE SHADOWS by Ann Bannon.
                                         ISBN 0-930044-85-1   5.95

JOURNEY TO A WOMAN by Ann Bannon.
                                         ISBN 0-930044-86-X   5.95

BEEBO BRINKER by Ann Bannon.   ISBN 0-930044-87-8   5.95
        Legendary novels written in the fifties and sixties,
                set in the gay mecca of Greenwich Village.

VOLUTE BOOKS

JOURNEY TO FULFILLMENT   Early classics by Valerie   3.95

A WORLD WITHOUT MEN   Taylor: The Erika Frohmann   3.95

RETURN TO LESBOS   series.   3.95

These are just a few of the many Naiad Press titles — we are the oldest and
largest lesbian/feminist publishing company in the world. Please request a
complete catalog. We offer personal service; we encourage and welcome direct
mail orders from individuals who have limited access to bookstores carrying
our publications.